ONE NIGHT
WITH A COWBOY
PAINT RIVER RANCH

ONE NIGHT
WITH A COWBOY

PAINT RIVER RANCH

ELIZABETH
OTTO

Entangled Publishing
644 Shrewsbury Commons Ave
STE 181
Shrewsbury, PA 17361
rights@entangledpublishing.com

Indulgence is an imprint of Entangled Publishing.

Edited by Liz Pelletier
Cover design by Heather Howland

Manufactured in the United States of America

First Edition May 2014

For every city girl who found herself countrified, and for those who dream about it. Make it happen, ladies.

Chapter One

She was five-minus-two seconds away from throwing up. Grabbing the sides of the whirling carnival ride seat, Sophie Miller squeezed her eyes tight and dipped her head. She had no idea how her eight-year-old nephew Ethan talked her into getting on this contraption. A pile of puke in his lap was about to be the reward for his insistence.

Surrounded by tinny music, colorful flashing lights, and the smell of heavenly fried food, Sophie had been glad they'd come to the street carnival. She loved the noise and the smells and the crowd. It was the perfect way to spend her first night back in Montana in six months, giving her the opportunity to catch up with her sister, Carla, and Ethan, while relieving a little of the stress that had plagued her for the past several months.

And then Ethan had talked her into getting on the Scrambler, and suddenly the carnival wasn't so fun.

A hard lump burned in her throat, and Sophie pressed

a hand to her mouth to hold back nausea. Just when she thought she might lose it, the ride began to slow down. The milling crowd swirled and faded below her only to reappear again as their cart went round and round a little more slowly each time.

She tried to focus on the crowd below, hoping it would keep her lunch firmly in her stomach. A tall, broad-shouldered cowboy in a white hat and light blue shirt stood out from the mass of people surrounding him. The snippet of his face she could see as the cart whirled around became clearer on the next rotation when he looked up. He had a strong, square face and eyes that seemed to grab a hold of her, even from the distance. A long body with narrow hips made a drool-worthy contrast to the broadness of his shoulders.

Mmm, nice. Not bad for a focal point.

Since people-watching seemed to be helping her nausea, she was more than willing to keep eyeballing the cowboy. There he was once, twice, three times as she went around and around. Living in the city as long as she had, Sophie had no real experience with country boys and the cowboy's rugged hotness reminded her she really needed to make up for that. A one-nighter with a hot cowboy to remind her of the pleasures of life? Yes, please. Sophie admonished the thought with a grin and eye roll. That was the last thing she had time for right now, but as the thought skipped away, she realized her fear had, momentarily, lessened.

She found him in the crowd again and then, mercifully, as his image faded away once more, the ride stopped. Sophie's brain jostled inside her skull as she closed her eyes to try and find equilibrium.

"Coming, Aunt Sophie?" Ethan grabbed her fingers as he opened the cart door and jumped down.

She paused as the metal ride jiggled under the weight of its disembarking riders. The entire world seemed unbalanced as the dizziness took hold, sort of like her life had been in general lately. The phone call she'd gotten from Carla three days ago, saying that their mother's health was declining, had rocked Sophie more than losing her job as a paramedic a few months ago. The ride had given her a few terror-induced moments to forget why she'd really come to Montana, but that reprieve was short-lived.

Especially since standing right now seemed detrimental to her health and possibly everyone around her if her stomach let loose. She glanced around, looking for her hot-cowboy focal point, but he was gone. With a frown, she stepped down and sighed when she felt solid ground beneath her feet. A group of kids raced past her to climb onto the ride, and Sophie let out an amused breath. Twenty-nine and she still hadn't conquered motion sickness. The fact that she hadn't actually thrown up on Ethan, though, made her feel like maybe she finally had.

Take that, stomach! She mentally high-fived herself and unsteadily followed Ethan through the crowd. Ethan pulled her hand and urged her to walk faster. Sophie pulled back to rein him in a little — faster wasn't going to happen.

"There's mom." He called out for her and waved to catch her attention. Sophie squinted, Ethan's slight form suddenly fuzzy like a blotchy oil painting. Sounds rushed her ears, lights from the overhead poles were suddenly blinding. A cramp stabbed through her gut, making her dizzy. Six years of riding in the back of a speeding, bumping ambulance as a metro paramedic and she couldn't handle one silly carnival ride? There was something seriously wrong with that little twist of irony.

Sophie made out her sister's form and groaned, recognizing Carla's trademark impatience despite the distance between them. Carla was waiting near the mini-doughnuts truck, one hand on her hip.

Sophie gave Ethan a half-hearted wave. "Go ahead. Tell your mom I'll catch up. I just need to…" Ethan took off for his mom before she could finish. He knew better than to keep Carla waiting. Smart boy. Judging by Carla's stance, Sophie considered motion sickness a good trade for a few minutes away from her controlling sister. There was a reason she and Carla lived thirteen hundred miles apart and in the few hours since they'd been reunited Sophie had been reminded why. Cats and dogs had nothing on their relationship.

A twisting knot of pain made her middle clench. Sophie closed her eyes and took a deep breath, mindful of the people walking around her. She moved to the side where the crowd was thin and her foot caught on something hard and unyielding. Her body tilted backward, once again thrust into quick motion that sent her brain into a tailspin. Firm hands caught under her arms just before her butt hit the ground.

Instead of the dirt-meet-posterior slam she was expecting, she was lowered down gently. Her left hand instinctively reached out, grabbing onto the nearest object for support. Denim. Warm, soft, well-worn denim. Before she could register any more, a haze of stars exploded behind her eyes.

A deep chuckle and silky voice floated down as she lay on the ground.

"I'm used to women throwing themselves at me, but this was a little fast, don't you think?"

• • •

This was turning into a helluva good day. Tucker Haywood flipped a toothpick from one side of his mouth to the other. When his client had wanted to meet here to let his kids run around while he and Tucker talked business, Tucker had initially resisted. It was a carnival—loud, flashy, and crowded. Everything he hated. He'd rather stay home at Paint River

Ranch and hold the meeting in his office. But if going to the carnival meant selling a horse, he'd relent and collect a big, fat check for his trouble.

Now he had a beer in one hand and a pretty woman at his feet.

Go figure.

He'd noticed her on the ride, even chuckled at the comical grimace on her face while the boy sitting next to her had clapped and whooped as the contraption flew by. Tucker had almost walked away, but then he noticed her eyes latching onto him. Not just once, but each time the ride went 'round. Something about the stubborn, albeit nauseated, expression on her face made him hang around until she got off the ride. He wasn't looking for a woman tonight, but it had been a while since he'd had a little female company, even if it was just for a drink and a laugh.

Noticing how green she looked just now, Tucker figured he'd be lucky to get that far. A white tube-top dress clung to full breasts and narrow waist, the hem stopping just above her toned legs that shone golden in the overhead light. A yellow string that peeked out from beneath the dress and tied around her neck promised a rocking bikini underneath. Light freckles dotted a straight nose and heart-shaped face. She was pretty, even with her eyes clenched tight and her full lips pinched white. It might even be worth getting puked on to find out a little more—especially if there *was* a bikini involved.

Tucker hunkered down next to her on one knee. "Hey, I was just kidding. You all right?"

She grimaced. "I'm dying."

Tucker grinned. "You're not dying." He nudged her arm with his hand, her skin warm and silky to the touch. The ride next to them dotted her hair and dress with bright polka dots of multi-colored lights. "Can I help you up?"

Her eyes widened. "Are you crazy? I'm dying here!" The left side of her mouth tugged up in what might have been a smile trying to bloom. A zing of warmth shot straight through him. Pretty and feisty—a dangerous combination because he liked both.

He tipped his hat back and shrugged, giving in to the urge to tease her a little. "It was just a ride."

She pulled her arm away from her face and pushed up on her elbows. Color seeped back into her skin. *Thank goodness.* But just when he thought she was on her way to recovery, a sudden frown clenched her face and she lay back down.

"That ride is the devil. I need some Zofran." She flipped off the six-armed, silver Scrambler that swirled in a tangled mess of chairs and bodies. Tucker chuckled at the unexpected gesture. Dimples curved beautifully in her cheeks when she managed a small smile.

"Hear that?" He tilted his head toward the ride where shrieks and giggles rang out. "I think those four-year-olds are laughing at you."

She groaned with a furious twist to her pretty lips. *Well, look at that little hellcat*, Tucker thought with an appreciative flutter in his stomach Yep, there it was. She riled up real nice, and dang if he didn't like the fire in her eyes.

"See how well you do in the hot seat, cowboy." She nodded toward the ride. "Go on."

Tucker reached a hand out and to his surprise, she took it. Her fingers were soft and warm. She trembled just a little as he carefully guided her up and his thumb swept the back of her knuckles, her skin smooth, her nails daintily curved with white tips. Not the hands of a ranching woman, that's for sure.

"I'm smart enough not to get on a ride like that," he teased with a wink, watching her closely.

She pulled her hand away, cocked her head, and smoothed

the front of her dress. "Meaning?" she asked, swallowing hard and picking grass from her shoulder-length hair. Her hair was two-toned, the ends a few shades lighter than the rest, like they'd been dipped in light blond paint. He swept his gaze over the length of her, drinking in the bracelets dangling on her right wrist, the bright red polish on her toes, and the shiny little blue purse slung over her shoulder. Everything about her screamed city girl. Tourist, most likely. She was the complete opposite of the women he was usually attracted to, but it was there. Attraction—pure and insistent.

He flicked his toothpick. City girl or not, she had his attention. All of it.

He smiled wide. "Meaning, I'm smarter than you, apparently."

Her arms crossed. "Are you smart enough to get lost before I punch your wise-ass mouth?" There was humor behind the challenge and, with just a little more ribbing; he might coax a full smile out of her. He liked spirited things for the most part: hard-to-handle horses, ornery cows, and the unpredictable Montana weather. It made life interesting and kept his restlessness in check.

He never was one to back down from a challenge.

"Honey, anything you want to do with my mouth is fine by me," he drawled, giving her a once over that he wouldn't have been able to avoid if he'd tried. Which he didn't. She gave him a long, hard look before a slow smile tipped up her lips. His hand itched to touch her, run a thumb over that full lower lip. There'd be a million and one ways to set off fireworks with a woman like her. Tucker bit down on the toothpick and reined in the thoughts making his blood hot. Something in the crowd caught her attention—a woman standing with a young boy across the crowd gave a wave. She gave an encouraging wave back, in the kind of way that said she'd catch up later.

Turning back to him, her gaze roved over his chest and down his middle, pausing at his thighs before flicking back up to his face. Tucker heated under the intensity of her appraisal—not realizing he'd been holding his breath until his chest started to ache.

The woman couldn't handle a carnival ride, but had no qualms giving him a blatant once-over. He was used to women looking his way—never had trouble finding a little company when the inclination arose. In the past few months, the female attention he usually craved left him unsatisfied and uninterested. Until right now. He'd been holed up at the ranch too long, and this silky, curvy, hot-tempered beauty had his interest by the balls, and then some.

"How about I buy you another drink?" she offered, tilting her head toward his beer. "That should keep your mouth busy for a while." She smoothed one hand over the back of her hair.

Oh, yeah. Coming to the carnival had definitely been a good call.

Tucker put a hand on the small of her back. Sweet warmth met his fingers, driving him to draw his hand up the fabric of her dress to the bare skin of her shoulder blade. He paused for a fraction of a second to see if she'd shy away from his touch. She didn't.

Tucker leaned close to her ear. The curve of her neck was delicate and beautiful, her skin radiated heat. Notes of coconut wafted from her hair.

His voice dipped low. "And when that's gone? Then what?" He steered her away from the ride.

She leaned toward him, as if pulled by his touch or his voice—maybe, hopefully, both. A soft rise of goose bumps lit along her back, followed by a gentle shudder. The smile on her lips promised everything he told himself he wanted to avoid. No more complicated one-night stands. No more messy, near-miss relationships. He was alone for a reason, though the sultry sapphire color her eyes had become made him forget exactly why.

She bumped against his shoulder. The heat of her body seeped through the fabric of his shirt, giving him a hard internal tremble and driving home what he wanted.

Her. Under him.

She smiled sweetly, gripping his shirt hard. "Don't worry, cowboy. I'm sure we'll think of something."

Chapter Two

When she'd left St. Paul, Minnesota two days ago, Sophie figured her fate in Missoula, Montana was pretty well pre-determined: be weighed down by guilt over her mother's medical condition, and fight over a constant stream of stupid nothingness with her sister, Carla, as usual. Both proved true in the first hour she'd parked on Montana soil. She and Carla had never been particularly close; they were on opposite ends of the personality spectrum. When they combined, it usually resulted in a nuclear explosion.

Carla was never shy about reminding her how disappointed she was that Sophie didn't come to Montana more to help with their mother. Sophie didn't bother to remind her sister that she'd been working overtime in Minnesota in order to help pay for their mother's medical bills, leftover credit card balances, and other expenses. Simply packing up and leaving her jobs hadn't been feasible, but now that downsizing in the hospital system had robbed Sophie of her highest-paying gig, she wasn't sure what to do. Her jobs had been her security, something she needed to function.

She'd had an interview at the Minneapolis Children's Hospital for a unit coordinator position. If she landed that job, which would begin in a month, she was definitely going back. Something had to crop up soon. She'd used almost all of her savings to stay afloat after being let go.

Oh, life and its troubles. Thank goodness the hot cowboy next to her offered a very delectable distraction. She snuck him a look as they meandered up to the beer tent. The top of her head barely came to his chin and, if the impressive breadth of his shoulders and bulge of bicep under the pale blue shirt were any indication, the man was built hard. When he turned a little and gave her a perfect view of the strength of his back and tight ass, she had no doubt.

"What'll ya have?" he glanced at her over his shoulder and Sophie's insides melted a little. His slightly downturned eyes had a sleepy vibe, the irises an unusual swirl of dark emerald and blue. He flicked the toothpick over a pouty lower lip. His chin was pointed, nose straight with a blunt tip, his jaw strong and covered with a whisper of dark brown stubble. Self-doubt echoed inside her; he was tempting, and she really, really should be high-tailing it out of there. Her time in Montana would likely be short, and the last thing she needed was additional baggage when she returned to Minnesota. But when his brows raised, his lips curving into a crooked smile, it was a definite stay.

Damn.

"Budweiser," she managed. He gave an approving nod, turning around a few moments later with two full plastic cups.

"Cheers." He raised his glass.

A chunk of mahogany hair peeked out from under his hat. Sophie's mouth went dry. "To?"

"To you, for being the best part of my day." He tapped his glass against hers. Sophie laughed behind a sip.

"Oh, you're smooth." She licked a drip of foam off the

lip of the cup. He tracked the movement, the light in his eyes getting darker. He took a sip from his cup, never taking his gaze from hers.

"Canadian." He said pointedly.

Sophie frowned. "Hmmm?" She took another sip. She couldn't remember the last time she'd had a beer. Wine was her usual, but she regretted that a little because the beer was foamy heaven on her tongue.

"Your accent sounds Canadian."

"Nope. But I get that a lot." His face displayed that his mind was working out other possibilities as they walked out of the tent area and into the melee of carnival-goers. Music blasted from a band on stage mixed with the varied tinkling jingles of the rides.

"Wisconsin!" he smiled, proud of himself. That smile was cocky and sexy as hell.

"Hate to disappoint you, cowboy, but no. One last guess." Was she flirting? It had been so long since she'd engaged socially with a man, she'd almost forgotten how. Sophie took a shaky drink.

"Do I win a prize if I'm right?" Smoke filled his eyes, turning the green/blue to an earthy dark shade. She didn't answer, just mentally rolled around in the sensual look on his rugged face. Sophie's neck burst into tingles and, despite rubbing a palm there, the sensation didn't go away.

He took another drink. "Minnesota."

Sophie saluted him with her cup, barely able to catch her breath to form words. "Ding, ding. You win. Very good."

He smiled around the toothpick. She tried to look away, but brain and body communication was having a small malfunction. Back home, men mostly came from one of three groups: businessman, college student, or hipster. There were a few other types scattered into the mix, but no cowboys. From the stark white hat, to the dark jeans and the polished silver belt buckle that shone in the light enough to give a girl glitter-envy, this man pulled off cowboy really well.

He bumped into her arm, sending fire through her body. Sophie stumbled, sloshing beer on the ground. One big hand wrapped around her upper arm to steady her. She smiled up at him, feeling silly and way too flustered. She'd never been one to shy away from men, but lately, a date or even a passing thought of a hook-up had been the farthest thing from her mind. Stress made some people find randy outlets, like too much sex or alcohol. Her? She holed up in her apartment and stared at the television. She preferred to be alone when she was crabby and stressed—just her and the occasional cheap bottle of Arbor Mist.

Little fingernails of panic streaked down her spine at the hard warmth of Tucker's touch. There was something sublimely familiar about this cowboy, and it caused a little voice inside her to scream *get back in the game,* instead of *run away, stupid.* His fingers slid away from her skin, leaving a singed sensation behind. She rubbed her arm more to capture the sensation than to scrub it away. Sweet warmth spread in her lower belly as Tucker leaned down to her as if he was going to speak. Sophie moved a little closer to him in response. It wasn't as if she'd come here looking for a man or a relationship. Hell no. She wasn't staying in Montana…so a little closeness with Mr. Sex in Jeans wasn't such a big deal, was it?

She was going with no.

"What's your name? We kinda forgot that part."

"Sophie." She noticed how his right incisor jutted forward slightly, adding just enough sass to his otherwise perfect teeth. It jacked his cockiness through the roof. They passed a speaker blaring music and she wasn't sure he'd heard her.

"Fifi?" His lips nearly touched her ear. The muscles in her legs turned pretty close to jelly at the near-contact. If what he'd said wasn't so ridiculous, her body might have given in to the mush-effect and fallen in his arms. But she burst out with a laugh instead, shaking her head, as her body recovered.

"So-phie."

That crooked smile got wider. He thrust out a hand, wrapped his fingers around her palm. "Tucker."

Sophie groaned a little. Of course. A cowboy named Tucker who was hot as sin and probably an incredible eight-second ride. Wasn't that the cliché? Living in the city her entire life meant she knew nothing about country boys, but she'd take cliché if it meant finding out how real it may or may not be. He looked the part so well, she was betting on real.

They rounded a curve of games, carnies calling out to them to try a few plays. "So about that prize." Tucker's eyes narrowed. Her gut flip-flopped.

"Prize?" Mmmm, her nerves were sparking at the thought of what a Tucker-prize might be.

"For guessing where you're from." He looked right at her mouth, moved in so the fabric of his shirt brushed against her breasts. Her nipples tightened in response. Sophie sucked in a breath and moved to take a step back, but never actually made it that far. The thoughts rolling around in her head were sinful. And tempting. And, by the sexy expression on Tucker's face, highly possible.

"What did you have in mind?" She took a small sip to break the tension inside her. It didn't work. Tucker stepped closer and took her chin in his hand. His thumb swept across the width of her mouth with a barely-there caress. The noise faded into a hazy blob, the lights tunneled into little polka dots around them. He stepped one breadth closer, leaving no question of his intention, his head dipping low. He was going to kiss her. She shouldn't, really, but she was going to let him.

Oh yes, she was going to let him.

"Sophie!" Her sister's irritated voice pulled Sophie back from the edge. She jerked away from Tucker as Carla nearly body-slammed them, pulling Ethan behind her. "I just called your cell."

Before she could answer, Carla gave Tucker a distasteful once-over. "Hello." She turned wide, accusing eyes on Sophie. Forcing her irritation down, Sophie wet her lips to keep from screaming. She wouldn't make a scene in front of Tucker, no matter how much she might want to ram her fist in her sister's face.

Funny how fast my sister can push my buttons.

"Sorry," Sophie said neutrally. "I didn't hear it over the noise." She gave a small smile, but there was no diffusing Carla when she got like this.

"Sure," Carla snapped. "You were *busy*."

Sophie chose to ignore the juvenile whine in her sister's voice. "Carla, I'm—"

"We're leaving."

Sophie rubbed her mouth with a hand, glancing at Tucker. He sipped his beer, watching the show with an inscrutable expression. To say this was embarrassing was an understatement. Sophie wanted to sink into the beer-soaked dirt and wave good-bye to the world. But as much as she knew she shouldn't stay, she didn't want to go. She needed some space after the long cross-country drive and the emotional flurry of the day. Whatever was going on between her and Tucker was alluring and warm and she needed that, too.

"I know my way. I'll walk home later." She'd been visiting this neighborhood three times a year for the past two years. Navigating her way back to Carla's wasn't a problem. Sophie squared her shoulders and faced Carla down. Her sister's lips went rigid.

"Its fine, Carla." She insisted. "Go ahead and take Ethan home." Her sister shuffled a foot, maybe she stomped it.

Sophie frowned in distaste. Despite being nearly forty, Carla was great at acting like a child.

"So-*phie*, you can't go wandering around a strange city. You have no idea what might…"

Tucker cleared his throat and slid an arm around Sophie's waist. She jumped at the unexpected contact, but found herself leaning into him. "I'll make sure she gets home." His voice was low and steady, the tone shocking in its finality. The protective edge to his tone unleashed a sensual longing deep in Sophie's middle. Her shoulder pressed more firmly against Tucker's side. Carla eyed them both, and then glanced at Ethan.

"Fine. But I'm locking the door. Keep your cell handy in case you need it." She eyed Tucker pointedly before stomping off. Ethan glanced over his shoulder and waved. Sophie watched them disappear behind a row of tents.

Tucker let out a low whistle, tipping his hat back a little. "Your sister?" Sophie nodded.

Tucker gently gripped the fabric at her lower back. If her brain gave off any warning signals at all, Sophie didn't hear them. A boon of danger sirens probably wouldn't have done a thing. He had a comfortable ease that made him seem like a long-time friend.

"For your sake, I hope that's your only sib—"

Sophie reached up on tiptoe, pulled the toothpick from his mouth and tossed it. "Shut up and kiss me."

Chapter Three

Her lips were cool, but her mouth was hot, and the wicked opposites uncurled the little demon inside Tucker that demanded to be let out. The demon that wanted control, to gather her hard and steady in his arms, and trail his mouth all over her body. Sophie's soft kiss and the light caress of her fingers over his neck called to Tucker in a way he couldn't explain. Like two halves coming together. She was an out-of-towner, no doubt about it. Chances were, he'd never see her again, which meant he didn't have to worry about either of them wanting more than one night.

He let her claim his mouth, momentarily forgetting they were standing in the middle of a crowded carnival. She fingered the nape of his neck, raising scorching tingles where she touched. When her teeth nipped his lower lip with the whisper of a touch, Tucker pulled back. If his jeans fit any smaller, he'd have a hell of a time walking out of here.

"Sophie."

"I'm sorry." Her voice wasn't very convincing, leading him to believe she wasn't sorry one bit. Sophie touched her lower lip with her fingers and, for a moment, he thought she was going to wipe his kiss away. He was ridiculously glad when she didn't. Tucker gripped her upper arms, smoothing his palms down the length to her elbows. Her bare flesh quivered under his hands.

"That's too bad, because I'm not."

That independent streak she'd displayed earlier seemed to have slipped away, leaving behind a softer, vulnerable version of her. He paused, hoping she wasn't about to get regretful over one little kiss. He'd spent the majority of his life keeping other people's emotions at arm's length and he wasn't about to embrace them now, no matter how alluring Sophie might be. When she glanced up with a radiant smile, relief flooded him with the shocking realization that he hadn't wanted to end their time together so soon.

"I don't usually go around kissing strange cowboys." Her voice was thick with a chuckle that warmed him. He brushed her hair over one shoulder, so tempted to pull her back in and pick up where they'd left off. He traced the yellow bikini string with two fingers, relishing the way she shuddered under his touch.

"Nah, it's normal. I have that effect on women."

"Wow!" She laughed. "Cocky, much?"

"Nope. Confident. Big difference." Before she could reply, he looped her arm through his and led her through the crowd. "So." He glanced down at her, glad to see her face was still relaxed. "Too scared to get on another ride?"

"What?" Her fingers gripped his arm. He indicated to the left with a tip of his chin. Her eyes slid that way, her body tensing when she noticed the Ferris wheel. She was going to refuse; would probably say it was time for her to get going. Tucker's eyes narrowed just a bit. It would probably be better that way. Sophie was not his normal type, but hell if he didn't enjoy having her next to him. He did, too much apparently, since his brain was tiptoeing past the one-night only rule and conjuring up a plan to ask her out.

He didn't date. What was he thinking? Having his heart run through a grinder and handed to him on a silver platter three years ago was enough of a reminder why he didn't pursue anything beyond a one-night stand. And even those were turning into too much trouble. That he was forgetting his own rule right now was as concerning as it was terrifying. Still, he didn't want to let Sophie walk away.

"You really want to get puked on, don't you?" Her voice pulled him back. Sophie made a half turn to look at the Ferris wheel head on, giving Tucker a view of the long column of her throat, and the softly defined rise of her cheekbone and delicate jaw. Her toned arms crossed over her soft breasts, the feminine curve of her back leading to hips he wanted to trace with his palms.

"Okay." Her voice was soft, but resolute.

"Hmmm?" Tucker drifted with the unwelcome thoughts rolling around in his head. "Yeah." He snapped out of it. "Ok, come on." He urged her forward, but her feet didn't move. Tucker gave her hand an encouraging tug and she hurried forward.

"You won't get sick." He gathered her against his side, liking how easily she leaned in to let him support her as he bought two tickets. Her shoulders tensed and he was pretty sure she was talking herself into getting on. The way her brow dipped and her lips jerked to one side was comical and cute. And sexy.

"How can you be sure?"

"I'm confident, remember?"

She shook her head. "Cocky." A few minutes later, they were seated. Sophie wedged against his hip like they'd been plated together, her fingers digging into his bicep with a death grip. He gently removed her hands as the wheel started to move so he could slip his right arm around her shoulders and pull her in tight. A shiver went through him, like refreshing snow inside a cavern that had been dark and empty too long. She fit perfectly under his arm, her cheek pressed against his shoulder, fingers digging into his shirt. Even terrified, Sophie was perfect. Without giving it any thought, he snuggled her in.

He tensed when he realized what he was doing. He wasn't a cuddler. He could barely bring himself to offer his family members a hug now and then. The only female who got his undivided affection was his six-year-old niece, Birdie, and that was because she was wicked cute and irresistible. Family aside, he didn't get close to people. He supposed there wasn't any harm in holding Sophie for a bit. Not like he was going to make cuddling a habit.

The wheel went around three turns before their chair rotated to the very top and stopped. Lights from downtown Missoula were shinning below. Above them, the night sky was an expanse of black velvet punched with sparkling little lights. The moon and stars were brilliant despite the reflection of city lights that crept up into the ink.

"Sophie, look." Tucker tapped beneath her chin to get her attention. She didn't relax her grip, but moved her head to glance up at him. He pointed to the skyline. "Look."

She sat a little straighter with a soft exclamation that thrilled him. Encased in shadow created by the moon, a mountain range rose in muted black and dark blue in the near distance, two peaks reaching high and wide like spread hands cupping the crescent moon.

"It's beautiful!"

Tucker glommed onto his self-satisfaction. "I figured you get sick because you're scared. Take away the scared, take away the sick."

She looked at him with parted lips. "What?"

Tucker shrugged, giving her shoulder a little squeeze. "Are you scared?"

Sophie glanced around, her fingers loosening a little on his shirt. "N-no."

"Are you sick?"

Another pause and she smiled. "No." Just then the wheel lurched to begin its descent. She shouted and grabbed him again. Tucker laughed and held her tight, liking how her muscles were soft and pliable against him—how her tight grip on his arm made him feel needed. It had been a long, long time since he'd been needed by anyone but his family, or even wanted to be. He should have been uneasy right now, with Sophie in his arms, making him experience…*something,* besides just plain lust. He couldn't place what it was, not that it mattered. He was going to enjoy it before it was time to walk away.

This really had turned into a helluva good day.

• • •

Despite past experiences, Sophie wasn't nauseous or light-headed when they stepped off the Ferris wheel. Exhilaration pumped through her along with a sense of triumph that she'd conquered her fear, at least this time. Tucker's sideways, smug glances and crooked grin elevated her mood even more. There was a little boy behind that rugged cowboy exterior, she was pretty sure. Truth be told, she would have been happy being scared for the entire ride. Having her face buried in his shirt was a small slice of heaven. His chest was warm and rock solid and he smelled incredible. The fact that he'd made her comfortable with just a touch and reassuring voice floored her.

"You have cowboy super powers," she teased as they walked down an aisle of games.

"I'd like to believe I just have the special touch." He lightly pinched her upper arm with a wink. Heat flushed her cheeks. This was good. This felt good. She hadn't had a moment's peace lately. When she wasn't scrambling to find a job to support herself and help Carla with their mom's medical bills, she was agonizing over her dwindling bank account. It was time she did something for herself, and keeping Tucker's company a little while longer was it. The buzz in her blood wasn't from the beer, that's for sure. The sound of his voice caused that, and the tilt of his eyes and his clean scent of soap and spice. Tucker was a hot-cowboy cocktail and she wanted a narrow straw so she could enjoy him, and the buzz, as long as possible.

A streak of red raced by, ramming into Sophie's leg. A small boy in a red and black striped shirt bounced off her thigh, and landed in the dirt with an ice cream cone upside down on his chest. Sophie jumped, maneuvering her feet to avoid crashing over him. The little boy looked at her in shock, his arms going wide as mashed ice cream rolled down the front of his shirt.

Tucker knelt down. "You all right?"

Maybe six or seven, the boy steadied his lips and scowled, an attempt to not cry, Sophie figured. He took Tucker's hand and stood, peeling the ice cream off his shirt.

"Fine." He replied stubbornly. "'cept my sister is going to be mad. That was hers."

"I'm sorry. Did I step in your way?" Sophie dug around in her bag, pulled out a tissue and wiped at his shirt.

"No. I ran into you."

Tucker gave an approving nod and slid one big hand on the boy's small shoulder. "That's pretty honest of you to tell it like it is. Come on; let's get your sister some new ice cream." Sophie didn't miss the tender way Tucker regarded the child, his manner easy like he was dealing with another man instead of an eight-year-old.

The boy shook his head, brown curls flopping. "I don't have no more money."

Tucker urged him toward the ice cream truck. "Good thing I do then, huh?" The little boy smiled and Sophie's heart melted. She roved Tucker with slow eyes, clinging to the way the sight of him made her insides go crazy. When a flash of desire shot through her, there was no chastising internal dialogue to slow it down. She couldn't think of a single reason not to go with the ache in her body right now. Tucker was gorgeous, and kind and cocky and…amazing.

A few minutes later, the boy gave a happy "thank you" and walked off with two new ice cream cones. Tucker looked pretty pleased with himself.

"Ice cream, Sophie?"

Shaking her head, she caught his eyes and held them. His expression grew serious. He took her hand and walked backward, pulling her toward him as he moved them out of the ice cream line. Her heart raced as she licked her lower lip, willing her nerves to settle, knowing there wasn't a chance that was going to happen. She was jacked up; every part of her hyper-aware of the need he'd unlocked in her. Tucker had flipped some primal switch with his blatant masculinity and affectionate manner that called to her inner cavewoman. She couldn't look away any more than she could make the ache between her legs stop.

He gave her hand a firm yank, pulling her into his space where the heat of his torso washed over her. Sophie exhaled to steady herself.

"What *do* you want?" Tucker's voice was so low she wasn't sure she'd heard him. But then his hand cradled the back of her head, fingers running through her hair, and she knew she'd heard him perfectly clear. What did she want? How about a couple sweet hours in his arms to help her remember she was still a woman, a young woman, with dreams, and needs, and desires that had been buried beneath the heavy hands of responsibility and insecurity? One night with a sexy cowboy before she had to face her sister, her mother, and the reality of her life tomorrow.

Sophie stepped into his space and pressed against him. A low groan rumbled from his throat and straight through her chest. His fingers dug into her scalp as his lips pressed into hers, hot, firm, and heavy and exactly what she wanted.

What she needed.

Chapter Four

The amazing electricity running through him had to be because he hadn't had a kiss like this in longer than any real man would care to admit. He craved it. The way Sophie sank into him spoke more than her voice could have. She needed this too, it seemed. He liked her spunk and her softness and the way she took up a challenge, but she had a timid side that warned him to slow it down, even thought his body wanted him to charge ahead.

He pulled back. "Soph, are you sure you want to be doing this?" Tucker ran strands of her hair through his fingers. She looked up at him with a dazed expression, eyes heavy and clouded, her lips swollen from his kiss. *Not nearly swollen enough*, he thought. Hell, she was gorgeous and exactly the distraction he'd love to have tonight. Her wide, soft mouth and pert little nose gave her a feminine beauty he craved. But there was something about her, something he wanted to dig deep to reveal. Maybe it was the sound of her voice or the way she teased him; but something under her sexy layers resonated with him.

Sophie cleared her throat and he hoped like hell that he hadn't just ruined their time together. It shouldn't bother him if she changed her mind, but it did. Sophie would be damn hard to walk away from. She smoothed her hair with one hand.

"Yes. Do you?" Her fingers were still teasing the base of his neck. Tucker couldn't look away from the heat in her eyes.

He took her face between his hands. "Oh, yeah."

She lifted on tiptoes and kissed him softly. This was new. He usually did the chasing, the maneuvering, and convincing. He couldn't remember a time a beauty was ever quite this forward with him. When she reached up and kissed just beneath his ear with a breathy whisper, he nearly came undone.

"Your move, cowboy."

Tucker wrapped his arms around her, lifting her slightly until his lips bumped hers. "My move includes finding a soft place to lay you down, getting rid of this dress and kissing your body until you scream yourself hoarse." Her quick intake of breath fanned the demon inside him further. "If that sounds like the move you're after, then I'm all in."

Her body softened in his arms, and Tucker swore she melted a little. "Checkmate."

He set her down, grabbed her hand and twined their fingers. She giggled as he pulled her through the crowd, both hands hanging on to his. The gesture made his heart jump. He looped one arm over her shoulders as they left the carnival and stepped into the quiet street.

"Where are we going?" The unsteadiness in her voice made him smile.

"I don't know." He shrugged lightheartedly. He didn't. He hadn't planned for this. Usually, he let a woman take him to her place, but he assumed Sophie didn't have a place save for her sister's, and that wasn't going to fly. Tucker thought briefly to Paint River Ranch, but he quickly dismissed it. That was his safe zone, his no-one-night-stands-happen-here zone, and he wasn't going to let Sophie's sexy temptation infiltrate that. Tucker considered taking her to his truck, but then he saw it.

A hay wagon sat in shadow across the street, lined by a dark expanse of trees against the sidewalk. Probably used for giving rides to carnival goers earlier, the wagon was deserted. She caught his gaze, gave a sly, knowing smile, and offered no resistance when he pulled her across the street. When they approached it, Tucker noticed the interior walls were lined with a double stack of hay bales, leaving the middle open. They could sneak inside and be completely hidden from the street.

Tucker's fingers pressed into her chest, gently driving her back against the rear bumper of the wagon. He slid his hands down her arms, his thumbs smoothing over the backs of her hands and knew there would be no rushing this.

. . .

Just the feel of Tucker's long, hard fingers woven with hers was delicious. When he released one hand to curve it behind her neck and lift the weight of her hair, Sophie let out pent up breath. He was exactly what she wanted. Not safe. Not expected. Wild and sexy, and filling her with sweet anticipation that, for a little while, could make her forget so many things.

Tucker's head dipped fast, his mouth covering hers, leaving no room for reservations. Not that Sophie had any. She didn't. His hand left her chest to smooth around the ball of her shoulder, softly, with just enough pressure to let her know his fingers were claiming her skin. Then he edged her hips up and back until they slid deep inside the interior of the wagon.

Hay crunched beneath them as he placed one knee between hers, and drew her up against his chest. Aggressive and claiming, his lips parted and demanded even as she willingly gave what he wanted. His mouth was heady with the taste of beer and mint, an intoxicating blend that made her crave more.

Sophie whimpered in protest when Tucker pulled back. He licked her lips with the tip of his tongue and gave her a gut-wrenching, self-satisfied smile.

"I wasn't looking for this tonight, Sophie." He nipped her jaw, his hands burying into the hair at the base of her neck. All the nerve endings in her scalp raced to life. His chest rose and fell against hers, the movement intimate and promising. The buttons of his shirt would come undone easily. His skin would be hard and perfect under her hands, the muscles gliding and flowing with each movement. He had serious fire in his expression, dark, with an edge that clearly displayed he walked a fine line between control and letting go. A flicker of fear passed through her, filled with the promise of being taken, and of letting him. "But I'm damn glad I found you."

"Me too." Sophie tipped the hat off his head and slid her hands into his hair. The thick waves were the perfect grip between her fingers. She took his lower lip between her teeth, shivering as he growled. Tucker's hands braced her shoulders and nudged her farther back on the wagon. They edged behind the perimeter of stacked bales, completely hidden from view. The hay pressed against her skin softly rustled as Tucker laid her back, his body hovering over her with one arm braced on either side of her head. Every inch of him vibrated with intensity. Her body responded in kind, jacking the brazenness that was so unfamiliar, but so very, very welcome at the moment.

"I don't do gentle." The warning shot a hot ache straight between her legs.

"Then don't be." She took big handful of his shirt and ripped it up from the waist of his jeans. Tucker popped the buttons with one hand, revealing inches of hard chest that didn't come into view nearly quickly enough. His body was swathed in moonlight as he shrugged the shirt off in one swift movement. Sophie's insides incinerated at the shadow-highlighted outline of each hard muscle, his skin pulled smooth and tight over square pecs and the rippled outline of a six-pack she couldn't wait to touch.

"Holy shit, Tucker." She reached for the cut contours of his chest, her fingers tingling with anticipation of all that male skin. Heat radiating from his chest permeated her palms right before he gently gripped her wrists and brought her hands over her head before she could touch him.

"Hands up there," he whispered firmly in her ear. Her mind was clouded with the pulse of this crazy, wicked desire. Out here, with a man she'd just met but wanted anyway, in a hay wagon. A hay wagon…where he was pulling down her dress. God, she'd never done anything like this in her life, and each second brought her closer to the realization that she was very glad about that, because Tucker was the perfect accomplice to help her step out of her safe little box.

Cool air rushed over her bikini-top as he yanked the dress down to her navel. Her nipples—already hard as sin—were positively begging.

"I've wanted to do that since I first laid eyes on you." Tucker kissed her, one hand finding her breast and flicking the nipple through the bikini. Sophie arched into his hand as he deepened the kiss with a tilt of his head that meshed their mouths in a bruising connection.

Oh, yeah, she'd be bruised in no time. Bruised and happy if he kept this up.

Tucker untied the string around her neck, pulled the top down to bare her breasts. She should have been uncomfortable, embarrassed even. But she wasn't. She craved his eyes on her; craved his hands and mouth even more.

His lips whispered a path down her neck, stopping to place a hot kiss in the dip, before moving over her chest and between her breasts. His mouth claimed a breast, tongue swirling her nipple in hot circles. Sophie forgot to breathe. Her hands found his hair as he moved from one breast to the other, taking time to tease each until her head throbbed from the sensation. His hands moved to her sides, fingers hooking in her dress and sliding it down. He grabbed the sides of her bikini bottoms and slid them down with the dress, flinging both beside them in the hay. Sophie shivered. She'd never been undressed so fast in her life.

Tucker moved lower, his chest gliding over her nipples, his lips blazing a trail between her ribs, taking sweet time to kiss her belly while his palms pressed against her hips. He kept moving down, the soft hairs on his chest tickling her skin, until his hot breath washed over the apex of her thighs. Tucker's long fingers caressed her from hips to knees, and slowly climbed back up on the sensitive insides of her thighs. Sophie arched with a flicker of panic at the force of need racing through her. It was potent and maddening and insane. She wanted to touch him, to feel his skin under her palms and let his body anchor her into the moment. Right now, she felt wildly out of control, spiraling like he'd plunked her on the fastest carnival ride in the park and left her alone.

He looked up as his fingers brushed her curls. Sophie jerked at the contact with a little moan. His lips curled into that crooked smile, barely visible in the dim light.

"Am I going too fast?" Tucker asked as his fingers parted her. His head dipped and a stream of heat washed over her tender flesh. Sophie tried to respond, was pretty sure a whimper was all she managed. Arms splayed at her sides, Sophie grabbed fistfuls of hay. It scratched and poked against her palms as she gripped and released clumps of it and arched her hips. He took it for the answer it was.

His face disappeared between her legs a second before lightning heat streaked straight over her clit and forced fireworks behind her eyes. Blindsided by the pleasure, Sophie tensed in response. Tucker's hands pressed her hips gently down into the hay as his tongue laved over her with soft, long strokes. His fingers kneaded the tops of her thighs, sliding to her belly in soothing motions until she relaxed with a deep sigh.

Too much. It was too much but not enough.

Sophie lifted her pelvis to meet his mouth, loving the sharp prick of his fingernails digging into her skin while his tongue swirled and paced over her nub. Hay bunched and poked her bottom, but she barely realized it as a torrent of sensation built inside. Tucker didn't disappoint as he increased the pace to even, quick strokes. When she arched her back and cried his name, he marked circles of heat around her, pushing her faster, bringing her to the edge. Tucker nipped the tender flesh with his teeth, causing a sharp clench mixed with ribbons of pleasure through her center. Just when she thought she was going to fall, Tucker pulled back.

Sophie looked down at his shadowy form working such sweet, agonizing magic on her body. He placed little kisses along her outer thigh, to the knee and back. Nuzzling her curls with his mouth, he nipped just inside her thigh, quickly soothing it with a slow slide of his tongue. The ebb of pain and soothing calm barely had time to mingle when Tucker's tongue pressed against her again, pushing her fast and hard back into the tornado of sensation. Sophie cried out; Tucker chuckled.

And then he left her hanging.

Again.

"Undo my jeans," he demanded, kissing her neck with the glide of slick, wet lips. Barely able to breathe, Sophie fought the brain fog to do as he asked. She ran her fingers over his firm abdomen, desperate to touch him. Tucker grabbed her hand with a discouraging sound and placed her hand on the waist of his jeans. Her brain didn't want to take the time to figure out why he was so reluctant to be touched. She was too damn needy to care.

The belt buckle took more concentration that she wanted to spend, but after a moment, it popped open, giving easy access to the button and zipper. Sophie's palm brushed against the bulge of his erection through the denim. Her brain fog cleared up in a hurry. Just to double-check, she palmed him again. Her heart lurched. Nope, not dreaming. He was big everywhere.

"My purse," she flung an arm over her head in the direction she thought her purse might be. Tucker grabbed it for her. With a sly smile, she pulled out a small pink fabric pouch. Her friend had filled it with condoms and stuffed it in Sophie's purse. Just in case Sophie decided to have a little fun. She pulled out a pink condom, very happy for her friend's foresight, especially when Sophie hadn't imagined something like this for herself.

Tucker gave an amused shake of his head when she handed him the condom. Even in the dim light, it was hot pink. His lips moved like he was going to ask or make some smart-ass comment, but he refrained, took the condom with a wink and then pulled her right back into his intensity.

Tucker pulled his jeans lower and settled between her legs. Tipping her pelvis and supporting her hips, he nudged his cock at her entrance. Sophie caught his eyes as he slid inside. Her brain exploded in a cascade of sensation. This fullness, *his* fullness, was more than she'd ever experienced and the way her body adjusted and settled around him caused a cacophony of feeling.

His forehead tipped to her shoulder. "God, Sophie." Tucker sucked in a breath and held still to let them both adjust. His hands slid up her body to cup her breasts. Then he gripped her hands, twining their fingers again and holding them out to the sides as he rose a little higher between her legs, driving just a little deeper. Sophie cried out, her hips thrusting up in desperation. He needed to move, fast. Hard. To complete her before her brain exploded from frustration.

She almost begged, but then he moved. Slow and methodical so the length of his cock slid against her clit with each stroke. One stroke, two, three…it didn't take long before the spiral was back full force and carrying her away. Sophie wrapped her arms around his neck and cried out into his chest as the orgasm tore through her.

"Awww, Sophie," he growled, burying his face in her neck.

Tucker wedged her tighter against his thighs, pulling back and slamming into her. The force of pleasure riveted her in place, rendered her nearly useless to move, to do anything but feel. His teeth nipped her neck, his lips grinding into hers as he dug fingers into her lower back and came hard.

"Sophie…" He pumped hard a few more times, his back arched over her, his arms quivering. Sophie was sure a blast had gone off close to them, rendering her deaf and confused. Time and place ceased to exist. When Tucker curled around her, gathering her up in his arms, the world began to clear inch by inch. Several long moments passed before she could move or think. With soft kisses, Tucker lay on his side next to her. The soft crunch of hay pulled her to look at him. Their eyes met and her heart slammed to her feet. Tucker smiled slow and lazy, tracing one finger around her face and tucking hair behind her ear. She turned to her side, her middle full of emotions she couldn't begin to comprehend. How was it she'd only known him a few hours?

Tucker leaned in for a hot, open-mouth kiss. His tongue drew little circles along hers, fanning desire right back to life. Sophie chuckled, warmth spreading through her.

"Better not do that or we won't get out of this wagon."

Tucker touched her cheek, letting his fingertips fall over the crest of her jaw. "I wouldn't mind. Sophie, this was an incredible end to the day." He was beautiful. Even in the barely-there-light, the planes and dips of his face, and self-satisfied gleam in his eyes grabbed her.

"Yeah." They lay there a while longer, staring at each other in the slivered moonlight. Shuffling and conversation from the street made her take notice. "We'd better get out of here."

They righted their clothes and Tucker helped her out of the wagon, pulling her against him for a mind-blowing kiss. Sophie sucked down the rise of schoolgirl flutters in her belly.

"How long are you in town?" Tucker put a hand to her lower back as they walked.

Sophie shrugged. She'd be heading back to Minnesota as soon as she was sure her mother was going to be all right. "I'm not sure exactly, but it won't be long."

He paused mid-step and turned to her. "See me again." It was a demand, not a question, and by the slight quake in his voice, not one Tucker was used to uttering. A lump wedged in her throat. Sick mother. Bitchy sister. No job. No money. What a fine list of all the reasons she couldn't do this with him again. What was the point of even thinking about a relationship, even a mini-one, when her life was so complicated right now? No, this hook-up with Tucker had been perfect. The constant tension in her shoulders was gone, and all her muscles loose and happy, her soul lighter than it had been in a while. There was no sense in messing with a good thing.

"Carla's is only three blocks from here," Sophie waved the direction. Her body was thumping with a satisfaction that she'd missed so much. The sex had certainly been overdue, but there was a residual she wasn't used to—the sensation of connection, of fitting just right. Considering she hadn't had an explosive roll in the hay quite like that before, Sophie wasn't surprised her endorphins were pumping her with all sorts of tingly warm fuzzies.

"Is that a no?" The stiffness in Tucker's tone drew her out of her head. He waited for a response with the look of a man who was used to being answered—and getting what he wanted. But he wouldn't, not this time. Not with her, because she was so far removed from being relationship material, even if it was only for the time she was in Montana. She couldn't take on another complication.

"I can't, Tucker. I'm sorry." The sound of his breath filled the silence for two beats…three, before he let his hand slip away from her back, giving her a chill and an almost desperate, sinking feeling in her gut. The absence of his touch stung a little, but that was okay. Because they were ending this now, walking away from each other and heading back to their separate lives. When they made it to Carla's and Sophie stopped at the front porch, the cool, almost arrogant expression on Tucker's face made it clear it was time to burn this bridge. Good, he was on board with the one-time-only idea.

She pulled a key from her purse and unlocked the door, trying to think of the right thing to say. Before she could speak, Tucker tipped his hat.

"Have a nice night, Sophie." He spun, trotted down to the curb, and disappeared into the darkness.

Chapter Five

Two days has passed since the carnival and Sophie still had a sweet little ache between her legs and a tender hickey on the inside of her thigh. Tucker had marked her for crying out loud. And she'd loved it. Too bad that hot cowboy would forever remain nothing more than a delicious memory. Sophie smiled dreamily, eyes closed, and settled into the memory of hard muscles crushing her breasts and hay poking her ass. She'd replayed their time together over and over, waiting for some measure of guilt to show up, but it didn't. Sophie wasn't sure if she was more surprised over her wanton behavior with Tucker or the fact that she didn't feel bad about it.

For a girl who always walked the straight and narrow, she'd sure given up on being Little Miss Perfect. Maybe it was her subconscious' way of telling her to relax. Enjoy life instead of just struggling through it. Because it had been a struggle lately and, as she settled into the plush chair in the waiting area at the Pine Haven nursing home, Sophie had the heavy sense that the struggle wasn't going to get better anytime soon.

Closing her eyes, she relaxed into the chair. She waited for the nurses to finish her mother, Violet's, bath. They were getting results from the latest round of medical tests today, about the effects from her traumatic brain injury. Carla had gone to the guest kitchen for coffee, thankfully, giving Sophie a few minutes of solitude. Being under Carla's roof was an experience in extreme patience. Not only was she demanding and loud, she nit-picked her husband, Mark, to death. The poor man kept a great face during daylight hours, but the two unleashed under the cover of darkness, fighting in hushed, bitter tones. If she heard it, there was no doubt Ethan did, too. Sophie was happy to be leaving Carla's tomorrow for a short retreat. Her only regret was not being able to bring her nephew. Poor kid.

She sunk a little lower in the chair with an unladylike spread of her jean-clad knees and crossed her hands against her middle. She'd been tired since arriving in Montana, it seemed. Both her brain and her body refused to settle in. Sleep could easily wiggle in as she succumbed to the quiet around her and the cloud-like softness of the cushions. Her brain began a slow decent into barely-there awareness, the kind that teetered between awake and asleep.

A few blissful minutes passed where she processed nothing except the work of her chest as she breathed. Her thoughts slid into a breezy daydream where Tucker was wearing a highway construction worker's bright orange vest and a hard hat. He was bleeding from his arm, and Sophie leaned over him with gauze pressed to his wound as traffic sped by on I-35. He tipped his hardhat back a little, a toothpick jutting cockily from the side of his mouth.

She smiled; recognized the gesture in her hazy state. Tucker was in her world, back when she was working as a medic and had something that resembled a future ahead of her. When she had something to offer a partner and herself besides uncertainty…

"Good god, Sophie, sit up straight!" Carla whacked her on the knee with a newspaper. Sophie looked up to see a coffee cup thrust in her face. "Were you sleeping? We can go in now." Without waiting for an answer, Carla hurried off. Sophie took three big breaths, holding the hot white ceramic mug in her hands while her brain fog cleared. She wasn't going to think about Tucker or what-ifs. Those things were the least of her worries today. Today, it was all about her mom.

Taking a scalding sip from the mug, Sophie went to her mother's room. She'd come every day since arriving in Missoula, yet the impact of her mother's condition still felt like a frying pan to the face. Violet Miller had been a preschool teacher for almost thirty years, an avid gardener and hiker, and stubborn enough to beat skin cancer and a breast tumor. She'd raised two girls alone, absorbing the trials of teenage PMS, boy-drama, dance lessons, and prom with a steady grace that Sophie relied on so much. It took stepping in the wrong place while snapping pictures in Glacier National Park to bring Violet Miller down. The rocks beneath her hiking boots had given way, pitching her over a cliff. Five seconds and twenty feet robbed her of the most vibrant years of her life, and left Sophie and Carla with a shell of the mother they knew.

Violet never made it back to her home in Minnesota. Massive head trauma left her in a near-vegetative state, making a thirteen-hundred-mile transfer back to St. Paul risky. Instead, Violet settled into a care facility near Carla's home in Missoula. Sophie stayed in Minnesota, working and taking care of what she could of her mother's loose ends. Even now, almost two years since the accident, there were accounts to settle, insurance claims to fight, and a never-ending stream of medical bills that weren't touched by health coverage.

And Sophie missed her mom—her best friend—

relentlessly.

She sat next to her mother's bed. Violet was upright, her head lolled to one side, eyes closed. In the past year, her shoulder-length brown hair had gone completely gray. Sophie never imagined her mother would gray so early in life, she was only fifty-eight, and the shocking white seemed like another play of fate to strip Violet of her essence well before her time.

Carla bustled around the bed, straightening the sheets and smoothing the duvet. She checked to be sure Violet had the hand-knit bootie slippers on that her teacher friend from back home had made, and that her pink flannel gown was properly buttoned.

"Can't trust anyone to do a good enough job, right mom?" Carla asked, sitting opposite from Sophie. Violet moaned, her eyes rolling to Carla for a second before dropping back to the left. Sophie froze when her mother's eyes seemed to focus on her face. During her other visits the past two days, her mom hadn't made any indication that she even realized Sophie was there.

"Hi mom, it's Sophie."

Carla scoffed. "She's not stupid, Sophie. She knows it's you." Carla patted her mom's hands. "She's probably just shocked to see you. It's been a while, hasn't it mom?"

Sophie bit back a sharp reply. It was true. She'd wanted to visit more often, had even considered moving to Missoula during one of Carla's guilt-tripping phone calls, but her jobs as paramedic and an occasional dance instructor left her little time. After being laid off, she'd been too emotionally strained to make the trip. Thinking of herself, she supposed, but making the long drive with all the noise in her head had seemed impossible and unsafe. But when Carla had called to say Violet was worse, it had changed everything.

"I'm here for a bit, mom. I'll come see you more."

Carla shot her a scalding look. "Don't make her promises you can't keep, Sophie!"

Sophie straightened in her chair and tilted her head, her lips set defiantly. She was about to retort when Dr. Keen walked in with a file. Tall and willowy, Amy Keen had a calm presence and steady voice that fit her profession well. She pushed her glasses up from the tip of her nose and smiled.

"Morning, ladies," she said. Her reassuring voice soothed Sophie's frazzled nerves. Dr. Keen leaned over Violet with a big, warm smile. "Good morning, Miss Violet." Violet made no response.

"Carla, Sophie, let's chat in the family room." Sophie had met Dr. Keen several times during her visits here and had grown to admire the doctor's honest, caring demeanor. The physician's shoulders were set a little straighter as she walked them to the family room, her deep, bright smile less radiant than usual. A pang hit Sophie straight through the gut as the worried sensation she'd had earlier strengthened.

Settled in the family room, Carla poured more coffee as the doctor laid the file open. "The results of Violet's latest scan are here, and I'm afraid it's not good news." The doctor placed two gray and white images of Violet's brain side-by-side on the table. "As you know, she has an inoperable blood clot here and a pinpoint aneurysm in her brain here. It's been slowly leaking off and on, but has remained remarkably stable all this time. Except now it's grown in size since her last scan." Dr. Keen used a pen to indicate a small dark gray area on the first image. Then she pointed to the newest scan. The gray area was twice as large as the first. Sophie leaned in closer, dread multiplying in leaps and bounds at the image.

"This dark area here shows how much brain tissue has died since her last scan four months ago. The doctor believes she's had a stroke sometime in between then and now, and this damage here is the result." The doctor pulled the pen back and looked at them both. Sophie couldn't meet her eyes.

"This area here," she said, pointing to the new scan with one beautiful fingernail, "is the new bleeding from the enlarged aneurysm. So, what this all means is that the aneurysm is bleeding more than before, and her risk of rupture, massive stroke, or, at the very minimum, multiple mini-strokes, is very high." Sophie attempted to set her coffee mug down, but her hand wouldn't stop shaking and her arm refused to extend toward the table. Carla was silent, never a good sign. Sophie slid a sideways glance at her sister; her face was pale and drawn.

Dr. Keen cleared her throat and continued. "We can't say when a life-ending stroke or bleeding may happen. All we know is that it's inevitable and, unfortunately, there isn't any type of treatment that is going to make a difference. Keeping her comfortable is our main priority at this point. I'm very sorry." A soft touch alighted on Sophie's hand, but she couldn't move her eyes from the floor to acknowledge Dr. Keen's gesture. Inevitable. Of course it was; they'd known that all along. But there was always hope that somehow, Violet's body would turn itself around. They'd moved her to this care facility partly because of their advancements in traumatic brain treatment, but there was nothing they could do for her.

Sophie's eyes drifted to the wall, a bubble seemingly wrapped itself around her and lifted her off to her own little world. Her mom was going to die, the reality of that was much closer than it had ever been. All her life, Sophie had done everything right. Perfect grades, excelled at dance and athletics, aced her college courses, and landed a good job as soon as her shiny new medic license was in her hands. Then her world crashed. Sophie had been everything and now she had nothing. She'd come here thinking there might be some hope.

But there wasn't any.

Chapter Six

It had been four days since the carnival and Tucker was pissed. Paint River Ranch was a mess of activity and it dug under his skin so deep, he could itch down to bone and still not make it go away. Thirty-eight thousand acres of ranch squeezed him, nearly strangled him, and there wasn't a single place he could go that made any difference. He'd ridden into the mountains early this morning when the summer air was still fresh and crisp, hoping to dump the unease in his gut. It helped for a while, until he returned, the ranch coming into view and giving him a sucker-punch all over again.

The ranch was growing and not in a way that made him happy and excited. Their Black Angus cattle operation was at its peak right now, the pens and fields filled with the highest census they'd ever had. Beef prices were good at the moment, and that's what Tucker wanted to focus on. Not the fresh construction that marred the ranch as a row of two-story cabins went in alongside the existing row. They already had twenty cabins, and soon they would have thirty. In the past year, they'd erected a small office for staff to take reservations, and a commercial kitchen building with a gourmet menu and room service. Paint River Ranch had been catering to tourists for vacations, weddings, and retreats for years, but after being featured in several travel magazines last summer, business had peaked.

Seemed every suit in a fancy car wanted a chance to experience the "wild West," and they kept the place hopping. There was a constant melee of guests coming and going, event planners coming in for client wedding venue tours, and delivery trucks bringing supplies. Tucker could care less about any of that. He was happy burying his head in the ranching side of the business. If he never saw another bride or groom or tourist pulling in with a Mercedes, he'd die a happy man.

This land was meant for ranching, not catering to over-moneyed out-of-towners with the itch to play cowboy. Normally, Tucker wouldn't have a thing to do with the guest portion of the ranch. That was his older brother, Cole's, department. But since Cole decided to play ex-pat and go to Australia to visit his new wife's family for a few weeks, Tucker was stuck doing it all. And he hated every second of it.

Ranch hands were supposed to move cattle out yesterday afternoon, but got held up with a bulldozer stuck in the mud, leaving the holding pen closest to the barn overflowing with cattle. Only pure luck kept them from spooking and charging through the fence. With all the construction going on, the packed round pen was a stampede just waiting to happen.

Tucker flicked the toothpick in his mouth. Giving himself a moment to sulk, he wished his brothers were home. The ranch house was too empty. Cole, his six-year-old daughter Birdie, and new wife Rylan were constants at Paint River and he missed them. The walls were usually ringing with Birdie's non-stop chatter, and the floors littered with her dolls, plastic ponies, and stuffed animals. Tucker hadn't stepped on a Lego in days and he missed it.

His younger brother, Levi, was due stateside from Afghanistan anytime now—they were just waiting on official word of his discharge from the Marines. Levi hadn't been home in six years and Tucker missed him more each day—though he'd go to the deepest recess of hell before he'd admit it out loud. Maeve, their mother, was taking advantage of remission from multiple sclerosis and spent more time with friends, sometimes away from the ranch.

Tucker was a little lost without anyone to look after. For the first time in his memory, he didn't have anyone to worry about but himself. Hardly a day went by that Cole or their mother didn't need him in some way. Once everyone was home, life could resume normalcy and Tucker could get the hell away from needy tourists and focus on cattle and training horses and filling his days with the land. It couldn't come soon enough.

He clamped down on the toothpick as a ray of sunlight streaked down over the grass in front of him. Brilliant yellow, the color matched a certain sunny bikini he hadn't been able to get out of his head. Sophie had been one hell of a distraction, but it hadn't lasted nearly long enough.

He crossed his arms over the pummel of his saddle with an involuntary groan. She'd been fire and silk and comfort and passion in his arms and, for the first time he could recall, Tucker didn't want it to end. Hook-ups filled a need: sex. He never spent the night, never called a woman for round two. Yet, he'd broken his own rule and asked Sophie to see him again. Yeah, that hadn't turned out well. De-nied. Served him right for putting himself out there. He learned long ago that he wasn't nice-girl approved. He was too much like his father had been—temperamental and self-absorbed—and Tucker was pretty sure he was lacking a gene that let him invest in other people's feelings, just like his dad.

No, he wasn't good for more than fun in the sack. By all rights, she'd had been too good for him anyway. City girl all polished up with her pretty nails and colorful hair. He tipped his hat back as the ray of sunlight began to fade away. Nice girls liked him because it gave them the chance to live out their wild side before they had to put their church face back on. Sophie had a wild streak, she'd let it out, and he'd enjoyed the hell out of it. They both had, but now it was over.

Done deal.

Except that his body kept aching for more of her, and he didn't have a clue how to make it stop. In the four years since he'd left his fiancé, Jewel, he hadn't wanted anyone for more than one night. He scoffed and clicked his horse into a trot. It served him right that Sophie shut him down. It was a good reminder that he wasn't long-term material. He was usually pretty selfish with his needs and he'd never apologized for that. Women didn't leave him without a smile on their face, that's for sure, but he never left them wanting a repeat. Repeats led to relationships. So, he'd slipped the other night, but Sophie…she was a smart girl. She'd put him right back on track with her polite, "thanks but no thanks."

Tucker rode into the barn, ducking as he crossed the threshold. Now as early morning squeezed down into the heat of the day, Tucker was ready to get those cattle moved and forget about Sophie's long legs wrapped around him, her nails digging into his shoulder… Fuck. He shook his head. They had plenty of daylight ahead, and plenty of work to do, and he wanted to be far, far away from all the construction noise. Spotting his right-hand man and best friend, Jaxon Moore, Tucker trotted over and walloped Jax with his hat.

"Let's go!" Tucker stopped the horse just as Jaxon grabbed the reins. "We're getting the cattle out of that pen." Jaxon smiled, flashing white teeth in a way that told Tucker something was amiss.

"You bet. Except we have a small problem. Twenty or so yearling heifers got loose. Boys are chasing them up right now."

Tucker swore. Loose cattle meant he had a broken gate or downed wire somewhere. Once the herd was high in the mountain pastures, they were free to roam where the liked. But down here, where the place was swarming with people, they had to be extra careful about keeping the Angus contained.

"Where?"

"Guest cabins. I was just on my way over to help."

Tucker stopped Jax with a hand. "No, I'll go. Pack your gear. We need to move those cattle today. We're going up to Harker's Pass." It wasn't the highest pasture on their property, but it would take them up the mountain and demand most of the day. Exactly what he wanted. Tucker spun his horse and trotted down the aisle and out the back door. Mixing guests with everyday ranch work was something they tried to avoid, more for safety than convenience. All he needed was some little tourist kid to get run over by an errant yearling.

At the top of a small hill, Tucker looked down and saw the yearlings had been rounded in the grass behind the guest cabins. Two cowboys on horses and three herd dogs had them packed in a neat circle. Needing to be sure all was under control; he rode the length of the driveway in between the rows of cabins to check for any strays. Brady King cantered his horse around the last cabin on the left. He made two more passes around, repeatedly looking back at something Tucker couldn't see. He figured Brady might be fighting with a slippery yearling, but Tucker didn't see a dog. Paint River's heelers were herd dogs to the core. Where there was a loose cow, there would be a dog rounding it up.

Brady looked up when Tucker approached, a furious blush spreading over the younger man's cheeks. Without a word, he tipped his hat at Tucker and raced off to join the group. With a frown, Tucker rode over to the cabin. What the hell had that boy so damn entranced?

An Adirondack chair sat in a small patch of sunlight next to the cabin, and a woman in cut-off jeans and a tiny yellow bikini top, with sunglass hiding her eyes and a book in her hands, lay draped along its length. Tuck swept her with his eyes—he couldn't help it—noticing her toenails were glossy red. His brow fell. The color of sunlight… That bikini top looked familiar.

"I swear, you ride that horse by me again and I'm going to bash its knees in with a baseball bat." She lowered the book and Tucker's heart slammed to his boots. *Hot damn.* She brought one hand to her face, dropped the glasses and Tucker grinned. Well, well. Leaning low over the saddle horn with arms crossed, he winked, his pulse rushing like a waterfall.

"It's nice to see you too, Fifi."

• • •

Sophie squinted as a cloud moved away from the sun and dumped fresh rays over her chair. A big brown horse stood perilously close, a cowboy with a black hat and familiar, shit-eating grin staring down at her. *Oh my god.*

"Tucker?" She swung her legs to the side of the chair and sat a little straighter.

"What are you doing here?" They asked at the same time. He laughed and brushed his hat back a little with one gloved hand. Sophie's heart was rumbling at NASCAR speed, her mind racing with the impossibility of running into him like this. As if the past few days hadn't been taunting her enough with his luscious memory, and now… He was here.

"I'm taking a vacation. From my sister," she managed,

her smile turning to a frown. The cloud moved and covered the light, giving her a full view of him. Sophie's breath caught. His face was exactly the way she had been remembering it in her dreams, the sleepy-tipped eyes bright and heavily lashed, the kissable mouth holding a toothpick in one corner. His brown shirt was rolled to the elbows, long legs clad in light tan leather chaps that wrapped from hip to ankle in a loving hug. A peek of denim jeans and boot showed just beneath the edge. He was rugged, dusty, and the sexiest man she'd ever laid eyes on. The instant, demanding pulse between her thighs said that her body fully agreed.

"That," Tucker wagged a finger at her with a smile that reached his eyes, "is a very good idea." The horse shifted weight between its front hooves with a snort that made Sophie jerk. She glared at its huge, hard hooves and inched a little to her left on the seat to increase the distance between her legs and the animal. She liked horses—the plastic kind impaled on a pole that bobbed up and down to happy circus music.

"You work here?" She stated the obvious because she was at a loss for anything more intelligent at the moment. Tucker sat on the horse with an easy grace and commanding hand that displayed he was well versed in handling all that power beneath him. It probably took years of experience to be that comfortable harnessing in the will and strength of another living thing and making it succumb to your will.

Or maybe Tucker had the same affect on horses that he likely had on women in general, and they just did whatever he asked because, well, he was Tucker. His shirt stretched over his bulging biceps and dipped into the flat length of his abdomen; peppered stubble on his jaw glinted reddish brown in the sunlight. Yep, he was just Tucker, with a voice that had soothed her carnival ride phobia, and a masculine beauty that could probably make a nun burst into tears.

"Ah, yeah. You could say that." His words faded off a

bit as his gaze dipped to her chest. Sophie followed his eyes, forgetting her girls were barely contained in the little bikini top. She'd moved the chair to the side of the cabin, figuring no one would see her since it was the last cabin in the row and a wide-open field spread before her. Usually, she'd be mortified to be seen in the skimpy top, but not now. Not with Tucker.

"I thought I'd ripped that top," his voice dripped darkness, the heady vibration of each word spreading gooseflesh over her arms. Huh, maybe he'd been thinking about the carnival, too. The idea that, just maybe, he'd been replaying their time together in his head, just like she had been, made her flush clear to her toes. Without thinking, Sophie pinched her thumb and forefinger over the string near her shoulder and ran them down toward her chest.

"I fixed it. It's my favorite." She withdrew her hand, mortified when she realized what she was doing by running her fingers over the string—enticing him, teasing. Tucker sucked in a cheek, making a clear indent, while his lips went tight.

"Mine, too." He looked over her bare middle, swept his eyes over her hips and legs with a hot expression. Her skin tingled like it had been a physical caress, each inch graced by his gaze, begging for his fingers to follow suit.

"So, why here?" he straightened in the saddle and made a sweep with one hand. "Why Paint River Ranch?"

She swallowed hard to bring herself back to reality. "Oh, Carla and Mark had a reservation here for the week, so Ethan could take riding lessons and what not. But Mark had to go out of town, and Carla offered it to me so I could get out of the house for a while." No sense in telling him it was Carla's passive way of holding Sophie at arm's length, or that she couldn't stand to spend another night under her sister's roof.

Tucker cocked his head. The heady sexual tension

between them seemed to snap, leaving a cool residue in its wake. They were suddenly just acquaintances, not one-time lovers, with the awkwardness of a first date where neither of them knew what to expect. And if she was reading his body language correctly—one arm crossed over his body, head tipped down so his hat nearly covered his eyes—Sophie figured Tucker couldn't wait to high tail it out of there.

She'd already set him out of her mind, chalked up their hook-up to just that, with no possibility of being more. It couldn't be more because she wasn't staying in Montana, and she had nothing to offer him anyway, so his sudden lack of interest didn't matter.

Sophie pushed her ponytail over one shoulder and straightened her spine. No, it didn't matter.

"You're here all week?" A muscle in the side of his jaw jumped.

"Mmm-hm."

The ground sounded like thunder was trying to rise up out of it. Tucker looked down the path as a cloud of dust settled around his horse's feet. A white horse with huge black spots pulled up next to Tucker.

"Hey boss. Brady said you were down here. Everything all right?"

Tucker swallowed and his Adam's apple moved with a slow glide. He clenched his jaw. Sophie's brows rose when she looked at the newcomer. His face was chiseled, his lips full and soft. Violet eyes made a startling contrast against his mocha skin. Sophie followed the opening in his khaki shirt, his neck and the rise of firm chest muscles dark and supple and dusted with a curl of black hair. Whatever they fed the cowboys around here was working.

The man looked her way and tipped his hat. "Ma'am." Sophie crossed her arms over her breasts and gave a shy smile.

"Everything's fine, Jax. Ready?"

"Just waiting on you."

Tucker looked back at her and Sophie's heart jumped. That face. She couldn't get enough. She smiled though it didn't quite touch her heart, thanks to the tornado of excitement and longing and hesitation swirling around inside. Tucker was stoic, his face displaying nothing. She crossed her arms tighter, equally irked and curious over his sudden standoffishness. Fine. This was a shock to them both, but their close proximity didn't have to mean anything. This was a huge ranch from what she gathered; they could certainly stay out of each other's way.

Her brain agreed, but her body said *no, no, no*.

Tucker pulled up the slack on his horses' reins. "I'll see you," he said. It was more final than promising.

She shrugged. "Okay," was all she could manage. He spun the huge horse. She was tempted to peek around the cabin and watch him go, but couldn't get her quivering muscles to lift her pathetic ass out of the chair.

I'll see you? What the hell did that mean? Sophie leaned back against the chair and replaced her sunglasses. She'd thought coming here would help ease the tension she experienced at Carla's, the kind that comes from being around someone who consistently rubs you wrong. Looks like she'd been mistaken about that. All coming to Paint River Ranch had done was give her new tension.

The kind that comes from the one person who rubs you right.

Chapter Seven

The Paint River Ranch brochure in her hand spouted nothing but damn lies. Sophie flipped it over with a grumble. The smiling couple on the front was having a great time horseback riding, while a smaller inset photo showed a young boy fishing in a pristine creek. *The Haywoods welcome you to all the relaxation a mountain haven brings. Rest, rejuvenate, and let the Big Sky soothe your soul.* Lies, lies, all lies. She'd felt nothing but restlessness and nervous energy since Tucker had shown up unexpectedly. There wasn't a damn thing in this sticky-sweet brochure about how to handle an unequivocally hot cowboy that you never expected to see again when he popped up in the middle of your rest and tranquility. Relaxed? Hell no. Now she was just frustrated and horny.

Her little cabin was perfectly quaint, with its red-stained exterior walls, white trim, and window planter full of Marigolds. And the pine beadboard interior with an old, wrought-iron bed and huge red-and-blue braided rugs was better than her crappy apartment back home. Combined with the stunning mountains all around the property and stretch of flower-dotted prairie off the back porch, Sophie *should* be relaxed. Carla had insisted Sophie take the week-long cabin rental. Her, "get some rest" comment had been a little ironic considering their mother's illness made rest and relaxation impossible.

She stuffed the brochure into her small pack, trying not to mingle too much with the other ranch guests waiting in line with her. Friendly by nature, Sophie didn't feel up to small talk right now. It was hot, bugs kept landing on her bare arms, and the other guests seemed overly happy about the impending two-mile hike. She tried to be happy. It was exercise. It would help her refocus and forget about her mother's dismal prognosis, Tucker, and everything else making her tense. Reading didn't work. Trying to take a nap was useless. Pacing the cabin was getting old. And no matter what she tried to do, her mind kept shifting to the grin on Tucker's handsome face.

Over half the state of Montana was likely populated by cowboys and she had to run into the one she never thought she'd see again. The one she hadn't stopped thinking about in days. The one who'd robbed her of sleep and any moments of rational thought, thanks to the constant mental replay of hot cowboy sex in a hay wagon. It was pathetic.

She'd wanted to line-drive him right out of the saddle and jump him—if she hadn't been too terrified to actually get next to the horse. Growing up in the metro in an apartment that didn't allow animals hadn't left Sophie many options for experiencing critters. The closest she'd ever been to a horse was the carousel in Como Park. Farm animals looked cute behind the petting zoo constraints at the Minnesota Zoo. Beyond that, she'd fed the fish in her third grade classroom and dissected a pig in tenth grade biology. Ending up at Paint River, surrounded by nature and animals, was a turn she hadn't seen coming.

A young man in khaki shorts and black sunglasses came around to the front of the group and handed out maps while Sophie swatted flies and tried to wrangle her brain into a happier place. She'd be going to the nursing home to visit her mother later, and getting her mindset into a calmer place right now would help her deal later on. When a man and woman on horses rode up the driveway and got a little too close, Sophie forgot about calm and panicked, scurrying to the left to get out of the way just as the man pitched sideways, nearly sliding off. If he hadn't grabbed the horse's mane in one fist, he would have gone down.

Sophie's medical instincts kicked in when her eyes settled on the man's face. A gray hue lay beneath a pale face, cheeks puffed out trying to fill with enough air to keep the brain going. His chest worked hard, dapples of sweat glistening along his forehead and dripping down his temples. Forgetting the horse, Sophie strode over.

"Sir? Sir!" She had no doubt he was going to be a classic fainter in about two seconds. The man's eyes were far away as he wobbled in the saddle. Sophie's arms outstretched to support him. The map guy rushed over to help, but was too late as the man leaned to the right and slid off the horse. He was too muscular and stocky, his weight a deadfall as gravity took over and he landed partially on top of Sophie. The air squeezed out of her lungs, the man's sweat dripping onto her neck. Shocked voices filled the air, faces blocking out the sun as people gathered around. A pair of hands helped roll the man to the side so she could get away. Panting, Sophie wiped the sweat from her face and got to her knees, mumbling a "thank you" to the map guy, who had a deer-in-the-headlights expression.

"Jim!" A woman with blazing blue eyes spread her hands wide as she fell to her knees. "Are you all right?" Jim's skin was clammy, the pulse at his wrist was normal if a little slow when Sophie gave a quick check.

"Jim!" The woman called again, taking the man's face in her hands and urging him to look at her. His eyes fluttered open, his gaze fixed on the older woman's face. Sophie touched his shoulder.

"I'm a paramedic," Sophie said, swallowing back a bitter lump that rolled around in her throat. Am, was. Semantics. "What happened?"

The man's fit physique and full head of brown hair made it hard to tell how old he was, but she guessed mid-sixties. Despite the obvious care he gave his body, there was no telling what kind of medical conditions might have cropped up. Her brain was alive with all the possibilities, carefully narrowing them down to those that fit the best.

"Got dizzy. We were just crossing the river when it hit me. I…could barely hold on long enough to make it back."

"We were trying to get to the ranch house," the woman said. She looked over her shoulder at the small crowd of guests who were staring. The woman indicated to the map guy that they should start their hike and, within a few seconds, the crowd had cleared.

"Did you eat today?" Sophie supported the man's back when he rolled a little to the side and sat. His breathing slowed down, color returning to his face. After a moment, he shook his head.

"No. We were too eager to ride out this morning." He looked at the woman with an affectionate twinkle in his eyes. "That's probably what did it." Jim stood, much steadier than Sophie had expected him to be, as she kept one hand on his back and watched his face. His symptoms easily pointed to low blood sugar—sweating, paleness, fainting—but it could be more.

"I think we should call the ambulance for you, sir." He wobbled a little and Sophie held onto him more tightly. He gave a little laugh.

"Ambulance has to come all the way from Missoula, a good forty minutes away. Let me just eat a bit, and if I still feel off, I'll have Maeve drive me in."

Used to the city with an ambulance around every corner, a forty-minute response time for a paramedic was a primitive concept. What if something horrible happened around here? The medic in her wanted to dig deeper, but with a confident nod, the man took a few steps and started walking away. Sophie kept up with him, suddenly aware the woman was leading the horses along right behind them. Crossing a few feet of lawn, they were at the front porch of a huge log house with river stone foundation.

He sat on the steps, and patted Sophie's hand. "Thank you, young lady."

She smiled. "Sophie. And, you're welcome." She opened her mouth, wanting to ask more questions, to do a proper exam. The amused way he looked at her told Sophie he knew, but he wasn't going to allow it. He thrust his hand out for a shake. "Jim Gilfoyle. To make you feel better, I have an appointment with my doctor tomorrow. For now, I think some lunch will fix me up just fine." The gray-haired woman hurried over, relief flooding her face to see Jim sitting and talking. Sophie studied her face a moment under lowered lids, realizing there was something strikingly familiar about her.

"Thank you for your help," the woman said. "I'm Maeve Haywood, and if there is anything I can do for you while you're staying with us, please let me know." Haywood, the name from the brochure. Sophie nodded.

"Thank you. I'm glad everything is all right." Maeve fussed over Jim, helping him off the step and ushering him across the porch and through the sliding doors. Sophie watched them go with a little wave. This elated feeling of having just done something important was the same she used to get in her paramedic job—knowing that she had the ability to help—to possibly save someone's life. Sometimes things went wrong, and in the worst-case scenario, she couldn't help at all, but the drive to keep trying made the bad times worth it.

She turned and walked back down the flower-lined path. Sunlight warmed her face, the heat sinking into the deepest parts of her that had seemed cold for a long time. She missed this, the feeling of helping, the rush of having her skills tested. Budget cuts across the city had put a lock on hiring with many of the metro's ambulance services. She'd applied to a couple, but was met with same answer: hiring freeze. Maybe it was time to think about going back to school… Nursing, maybe. She could do that. Or moving to some other Minnesota city to find a medic job. Irritation gnawed at her. She was almost thirty—the age when she should be firmly established in a career and maybe thinking about a family. It was ridiculous, really, that she had to virtually start over.

Sophie trotted up the cabin's porch steps and went inside. Restless now, her mind swirling with possibilities she really didn't want to ponder right now, she went into the bedroom for a change of shoes and her car keys. She might as well go into Missoula to visit her mom. A little alone time with Violet, without Carla hovering over them, sounded perfect. She was absently flipping through her cell phone on the way back to the living room when she heard the crash.

Her scalp prickled as she looked up from the phone and noticed she'd left the front door slightly cracked open. Something banged from the curtain-covered closet in the kitchenette. Something big by the sounds coming out of there. Gripping the cell to her chest, Sophie tiptoed to the closet, made a wide berth around it with her eyes honed in on the curtain, and she grappled to reach a spatula that lay on the breakfast counter.

She gripped the utensil until her knuckles turned white. Damn Montana and its animals. She contemplated pulling the curtain aside with her foot when the something lunged at it from the inside. Screaming, she threw her cell phone at the curtain. Instead of warding it off, the animal went super-ninja on the fabric, seemingly unable to find its way out from underneath. Until a little black nose peeked underneath.

Chapter Eight

He wasn't going to go back to her cabin. Tucker rode an uneven line between being irritated and elated at seeing Sophie again. She'd rejected him after dishing out what had amounted to the best sex he'd had in recent memory. Worse, he'd *longed* to see her again, an unwelcome realization that punched the breath out of his rule to never see the same woman twice. He'd smelled the phantom coconut from her skin, her taste just a wishful recall away from his lips. Tossing and turning in bed each night from the constant replay of her body under his hands was real fun, too. Yeah, he was in unfamiliar territory and thinking he would never see her again made it a little easier to push her out of his mind.

Then she showed up at his ranch in the same yellow bikini that got him in this mess in the first place.

Jaxon had picked up on Tucker's angst in the blink of an eye over coffee at four that morning. Tucker considered him a third brother. He'd shown up at Paint River when he was thirteen, thrust into the Haywood's care by an anonymous "family friend." Maeve had been more than happy to take

Jax in and, being the same age, the boys had taken to each other like brothers of blood would do.

Though his friend tried his best to pry, Tucker kept his lips sealed. Talking about his attraction to Sophie would do nothing but keep her in the front of his mind, and remind him why he wasn't good for her. Thoughts he could do without, thanks.

But now that coffee and early morning chores were over, Tucker couldn't stop the itch to go to Sophie's cabin. He had the potent sensation that he was forgetting something all morning, but was so distracted by Sophie he couldn't remember what. Muttering that this was a bad idea, but ignoring himself completely, Tucker drove to Sophie's cabin as slowly as he could stand without his brain imploding. Metal poles and a thick coil of wire banged around in the back of the truck, reminding him he had work to do. He'd say hi, he'd stay a minute, and then he was out of there. An unsettled feeling tried more than once to sit on his back, but he shrugged it off. His insides were having an MMA fight, his heart taking a right hook and doing a back flip by the time he got to her door.

And heard her scream.

By the time he'd pushed open the cracked front door and rushed in, she was uttering muffled little grunts like she was trying to beat something to death. Tucker found her in the kitchen, a blue plastic spatula in one hand, the other clutching a wooden spoon.

"Sophie?"

She spun with a shout, the wooden spoon slicing down and whapping him on the bicep. "Tucker! I'm so sorry." She turned back to the narrow closet next to the stove. "There's a...something is...it's an animal. In there!" Her eyes were wide and frantic, the spatula trembling in her hand. With her hair strewn in some kind of braid that had come undone, her shirt falling off one bare shoulder, Sophie was a perfect mix of terrified and sexy. He took a step to the closet, his boot colliding with metal. Two stock pots, a sauce pan and a broken cell phone lay near her feet.

"What kind of animal are we talking about?" he slid the stockpots out of the way with a quiet chuckle.

"I don't know. It's big." She gingerly held the curtain away for him so he could peek into the dark space. Tucker took off his hat and set it on the breakfast counter behind them. Sophie peeked around his arm. He reached up for the pull chain and turned the overhead light on. The tip of a bushy brown tail stuck out from behind a broom. Tucker stepped just inside the small closet, turning slightly sideways so he could crouch down. He glanced up at Sophie as he whipped his T-shirt off with one hand. A sharp intake of breath sounded in his ear, making him smile. *Hmh.* Maybe she'd been hoping he'd stop by after all. The sweep of appreciation on her face went right to his groin.

"Hand me my hat."

She did, crouching beside him so her shoulder bumped into his arm, jostling shivers loose over his torso. Her face was intensely curious and a little afraid and he couldn't help being amused at her expense. "Good thing I got here when I did, Fifi." Tucker bundled the shirt in one hand, his hat in the other. "What you've got here can get pretty vicious."

"Really?" she squeaked, squirming next to his knee. He knocked the broom out of the way, and brought his hat down with one swift move. Rampant chattering and rustling ensued under his hat. Sophie jumped.

"Yeah," he grunted, shifting so he could reach in with his other hand and slide his shirt beneath the hat, trapping the animal inside. Turning the hat upside down, he kept the T-shirt over the opening and shifted out of the closet.

Sophie's cheeks were flushed; her mouth parted in

anticipation of what he'd caught. Leaning toward her on one knee, he moved the shirt just a touch. A rusty brown head popped through. She gasped, stumbling back against the breakfast corner, her cheeks flaming red. Tucker covered the opening back up, pushing the squirrel back down and keeping it firmly inside. He laughed low in his throat, afraid to let it out lest she start beating him with the plastic spatula again.

"Montana squirrels have a reputation, you know. Man killers, they say."

Indignation crossed her face and she scowled. Tucker lost it and laughed full tilt. Sophie, smoothed her shirt and tossed her head back, looking down her nose at him.

"A squirrel."

"Mmm-hmm."

"Well it…it sounded *bigger*." She cleared her throat, her eyes glistening with anger and a flicker of amusement. She crossed her arms, tapping the spatula against her upper arm. Tucker rose, careful not to shift the shirt. He didn't miss how her eyes raked over his bare chest. Maybe a hay wagon repeat was in order…round two. He almost growled at himself to scare that idea right out of his head. Round two? Ridiculous, no matter how hot she looked with her flushed cheeks and messy hair.

"Were you going to flip it to death?" Tucker nudged her with his shoulder to get himself back on track. When she twisted her lips, he wagged one brow. "How about I take it outside and skin it? Then you can cook it up for me, seeing how you're prepared."

One corner of her mouth tugged up with a dubious squint of her eye. "People do not eat squirrels!"

He scoffed. "Hell if they don't." As if understanding them, the squirrel became demon-possessed under the shirt, spinning and knocking against Tucker's hand. He went out to the porch and tossed it gently under the railing where it made a mad dash out to the field. Just to tease her, he glanced at her over his shoulder. "Well, there goes supper."

When he stepped back inside, Sophie was still by the couch with her arms crossed but the frown was gone. A smile lit her face and it took his breath away. Her full lips were tinted with the same gorgeous pink that flushed her cheeks. Tucker moved to take a step but stopped himself. He wanted to crush her up in his arms and…

The spatula wobbled as she spread her arms wide. Her eyes roved over him, spiking his urge to pull her close. "You'd be out of luck anyway, cowboy. I don't know how to cook."

He put a hand over his chest like she'd wounded him. She might as well of confessed she used to be a man. That would have been easier to handle.

"So…does this mean no pie?"

Chapter Nine

Sophie hoped Tucker would forget he wasn't wearing a shirt. Her palms tingled to feel his silky hard flesh under her hands. Tucker's body wasn't sculpted with hard-cut lines and ridges found on men with gym-membership bodies. Instead, his chest and bulging arm muscles were delineated with soft edges, the flesh pulled tight and supple over each natural rise, mound, and curve of a torso built from years of hard labor and strenuous work. The strength of Tucker's body was genuine and it was a physique no treadmill could create. It was a body she wanted to know every hard inch of. Repeatedly.

Tucker's presence helped soothe some of the panic pumping through her at the moment. The ease of his body's movements, the cascade of warmth from his skin, and hell, his scent, pulled her away from the fear of rabid squirrels. Pulling her gaze from his chest to his eyes was a struggle, but she managed.

"Pie?" she repeated.

"If you don't cook, then you probably don't make good pie."

She scrunched her nose. "I know how to go to the store and *buy* a pie."

"Pfff, no. That is not the same thing. I have to say, Fifi, this whole 'no pie' thing might be a deal breaker." His smirk mocked her and it was cute, the way his right eye squinted a little as he teased her. This banter was easy, playful. Pie had her suddenly thinking of brown sugar melting in butter, warm and sticky and sweet—exactly how her insides felt just then—with a homey warmth trickling down her throat, filling her chest and spreading to every inch of her extremities, her scalp and the tips of her toes.

Hot gooseflesh rose on her arms and a dart of panic dinged her between the ribs. Tucker was too tempting. All that solid male flesh, the dark edge of his voice, and the sideways smile were too much. She could fall for this man in the blink of an eye and, if she did, she'd fall goddamn hard. Her future was at a permanent stall with no foreseeable change; her heart was wrapped up in trenches of constant worry over her mother. There could be no falling, and there was a good way to prevent that. Tell Tucker thanks, walk him out, and shut the door behind him as he left. It was only fair to keep him at arm's length.

Sophie took a step back and cleared her throat. The prelude to walking him out turned into something else entirely when she opened her mouth. "What…what deal would that be?" Like it mattered. The longer they stood here talking, the more she was going to want him, so…

"I was going to ask you something, but…" He raked a hand through his wavy, auburn-to-mahogany hair before flipping his hat on. "I'll save it for another time." He turned slightly, showing off the smooth plane of his left shoulder blade. A flash of white caught her attention. Without thinking, Sophie's hand snaked out to touch him. She gasped.

"Is that a…a brand?" He stiffened the moment her

fingers made contact with his skin. She traced raised white scar tissue over his shoulder. She followed a side-by-side capital P with an upside down, backward R. The brand covered half the length of his shoulder blade. Tucker flinched at the ministration of her finger over the markings.

"The Paint River Ranch brand."

Unable to help it, Sophie traced the markings again. The skin had healed in a perfect ridge to create a clear, white design over his golden skin. "This had to hurt like hell." Before she finished tracing the R, he pulled away. He didn't respond, snapped the T-shirt and slipped it back on, much to her disappointment.

His eyes swept over her quickly, and then went back for a slower round. Her belly quivered when his gaze paused at her lips. Then, with a quick nod of his head, he turned to the door. She walked him out, flutters swarming in her belly when he stepped onto the porch. He was walking out as easily as he'd walked in. Something told her Tucker had had plenty of practice with that.

"Ah, thanks for…getting the squirrel."

His left hand clenched and relaxed, clenched again before he shoved it under the waist-band of his chaps. "You bet."

"Will I see you again before I leave?" The words raced out. Her cheeks went hot. This was not going the way she'd thought it out in her head. Smooth wood met her palm as she gripped the porch railing. Seeing him again would accomplish what, exactly? Sure, she'd been lacking in the male-company department for a while, which is probably why Tucker was so delicious. Compared to the double helping of nothing she'd had in her bed in the past months, he was pure divinity. That wasn't exactly true. He would have been Mr. Perfect even if she weren't in a dry spell, because it was pretty likely there wasn't another man out there who could rival him in the hot department.

Tucker pulled the toothpick from his mouth and tilted his head just right, so that were she to step into him and reach up, she could meet his lips perfectly. The little twitch of muscle in his cheek said he knew it, too.

"Do you want to, Fifi?"

Yes. No. What was the point in denying it? As soon as he went away, and she found herself, alone, in the tiny cabin, it would become painfully obvious how much she wanted to see him again. The quiet, the alone time…all that room to think, and ponder, and regret. She crossed her arms. Okay, fine. One more time couldn't hurt. "Only if you promise not to make me eat squirrel."

His face went impassive while he sucked in his lower lip and looked up at the sky with a frown. Sophie followed suit. It was barely late morning, and clouds had begun to move in. The warm, damp breeze hinted at rain. Maybe she'd been wrong to agree. As his shoulders stiffened a bit, and his jaw worked, Sophie figured he had other things to do—things that didn't include making the time to see her again.

She tried to wave it off before this turned embarrassing. "Really, though, no big deal if we don't…"

His eyes snapped to hers, the smile back. "Go grab a sweater."

"Why?"

"Because you get to see me again right now."

• • •

He was trying not to be an antsy jerk, but truth was he almost couldn't help it. That nagging feeling was back in full force, to the effect that Tucker reached for his cell phone to call Jaxon, and realized he'd left it in the house. There was no sense in what he was doing right now, that's for sure. Rain was coming and he had work to do. He was obviously missing something that would probably come back to bite him in the ass later, too. Yet, as Sophie's scent wrapped around him in the humid confines of his truck, Tucker couldn't bring himself to fully care about anything that lay outside the cab.

It was all he could do not to reach out and pull the band from her hair, let it tumble down completely from the messy ponytail it was currently in. He'd wanted to take Sophie somewhere private—it had been a whim, but he was used to doing what he pleased, when he wanted to do it. Tucker turned off the main drive onto a dirt path marked through the grass by the width of tire tracks. They drove farther away from Paint River and deeper into the completely untamed landscape Tucker's heart belonged to. The path narrowed until they were driving on nothing but unmarked land. The mountain towered on the horizon, a constant navy-gray mass. As they drove, the open land began to close as pine trees dotted the space and the grasses grew taller.

Her gaze was all over the landscape with an appreciation that made his chest swell with pride. The remarkable differences in the land, from city, to flat lands, to rolling hills, to primitive mountain peaks, still took his breath away.

"Where are we going?" she asked with a look out the rear window.

"Somewhere you'll never forget." A couple minutes later, the truck sliced through a path in the trees and into a space where the ground got softer, the woods thinner, and a pristine river drew a ribbon down the side of the mountain. The water flowed across a stretch of flat land before them and interrupted the road. Sophie straightened, her mouth gaping a little. Tucker smiled. The river was impressive, yes, but that wasn't the cause of her sudden smile.

"Wow!" Sophie reached for the handle as soon as he stopped the truck, throwing the door open and hopping down before he'd even gotten his seat belt off. She leaned her butt against the front of the Chevy, arms crossed, genuine amazement on her face as she sized up the bridge making a gentle arch over the river. Tucker moved next to her, hands in his pockets to keep from touching her.

"The floor needs a little work, but we can walk inside if you want." He gestured with his head and they walked over, side by side. The covered bridge was over a hundred years old, and as far as Tucker knew, the only bridge like it in the state. The waterway below was fed by Paint River, which gave the Haywoods a roundabout connection to the bridge, one they'd used to fuel their secret upkeep of the bridge's supports, roof, and floor over the last ten years. Peeling red boards lined the exterior walls and the roof was topped with row after row of weather-gray cedar shake shingles. It was a one-lane, forty-foot structure whose presence was all but forgotten. Locals barely remembered it was there and, with no clear markings to its whereabouts, tourists usually only happened upon it after getting lost.

Both were fine with Tucker. In the rare moments they were able to escape their father and the ranch, Tucker, his brothers, and Jaxon would ride their bikes the five miles here, fishing poles strapped to their backs, to poke around in the water and play pirates inside the bridge. That others rarely came this way made it all the better for four rowdy boys with overactive imaginations to do whatever the hell they wanted. Someone usually ended up getting thrown overboard into the water; Levi mostly. Tucker shook his head at the memory as they stepped into the opening of the bridge. Levi had been a scrawny kid; how he'd survived so many "accidental" falls off the bridge was a miracle.

Tucker showed her the safest path to follow and Sophie went ahead, trailing her fingers on the worn and cracked wood as she walked close to the wall. Above, intricately placed beams intersected each other to create a running V-shaped roof support while cross beams lined the walls to support the separated lower and upper halves. She paused in the middle, leaned over the waist-high rail to look at the river below.

"What's it called?" She looked sideways at him, her face radiant. It damn near took his breath away.

Tucker blinked. "Hmmm?"

"The bridge. Does it have a name? When I visited a friend out East the covered bridges there were named."

He moved next to her, leaned his back against the wall with his elbows on the rail. "Nope, not as far as I know." Daylight was threatening to fade from the accumulating storm clouds that cast the interior of the bridge in shadow. A slight breeze kicked up, driving Sophie's scent over him in a gentle cascade. His lids lowered, his jaw grinding in response. She resumed her steady perusing of the river and, for a while, they didn't speak. Tucker turned around so they were shoulder-to-shoulder, listening to the water trickle over rocks below. He filled his lungs with a huge breath of clean, mountain air and Sophie.

"So, what do you think, Sophie-whose-last-name-I-don't-know?" He looked sideways at her. She returned his gaze, gave a light chuckle. Warmth eased through him at the sound. He hadn't been this at ease with a woman in a very long time.

"I think it's beautiful, Tucker whose-last-name-I-don't-know-either." Sophie looked down, her shoulders slouching a little as her eyes rose back to the water. She shook her head wistfully. "It's really, really amazing here."

A bit of melancholy worked its way into her tone. She stared off into the distance, her smile smaller. What was playing with her emotions so much? He never wanted to know anyone's secrets. He could care less what made people outside of his family tick, but Sophie's mood change made him a little anxious inside.

He wanted to fix it.

God, is that what this feeling was—the urge to make it better? Ah, no. No way was he getting invested in whatever was going on inside her pretty head. He wouldn't know how to talk to her about it anyway, or make it better. He wasn't the knight in shining armor, nor did he want to be. Ready to direct his silly brain, he smiled wide and held out a hand to her.

"Tucker Ian Haywood. Nice to meet you."

She took his hand for a little shake. "Sophie Anna Miller. Did you say Haywood?"

"Yep." His heart fluttered. Well, the truth was out there if she wanted it. He didn't have a problem telling anyone who he was, but maybe she didn't know enough to figure it out. Being a Haywood was both a blessing and a curse around here. The blessing part was due to the ranch's stellar reputation. The curse part was that his father hadn't left a personal reputation near as good. The two halves clashed frequently, especially for Tucker. It sucked being the guy most like the man everyone hated.

"Related to the woman whose husband or boyfriend or whatever I helped?"

Tucker traced his tongue along the inside of his lower lip with a steady stare at the river. "He's just a friend and she's my mother."

Sophie gripped the railing and leaned back on her heals, stretching her arms tight. "Wow, you own the farm?"

Tucker's face went tingly. Farm. Please. "Third generation, yes, and it's a *ranch*." Sophie gave an impressed nod and brought her chest back against the ledge. Little patters broke the surface of the river as soft rain began to fall.

"Farm. Ranch. Same thing, right?"

His left eye twitched a little, the lightness of her voice letting him know she'd resumed her sunny side—the side that meant he was off the hook from trying to figure out what was upsetting her.

"Damn, woman, you know how to kick a man right in the balls, don't you?"

Her face was full of mischief. Soft breeze carried loose tendrils of hair away from her face and brought the heady scent of humidity and rain.

"Well excuse me for being a city girl." The quip was light, the way she pursed her lips, sticky sweet. "City girls don't get to see things like ranches, or…" she took a big breath that sounded a lot like longing. "This." Her arm swept in an arc to indicate the bridge.

Then she turned to him and blinked. "So, if I were to refer to you as a farm boy…"

His eyes lowered to her lips, made a slow rake over her chest. "I'd have to extract some kind of wicked revenge." She made a little "oooh" sound with a wink that shot fire right to his balls. Round two with Sophie Miller? Man, it was against all his rules, but that sweet mouth turned up like that, her tight little body all wrapped up in shorts and that sweater… what man would turn down another chance in her arms? He almost groaned with the thought, and turned his back to the rail and crossed his arms over his chest. "Thank you for helping Jim, by the way. He's been a friend of the family since I was a boy and he's, well, he's important to all of us."

She touched his arm. "You're welcome. I'm glad he didn't have anything serious going on."

When his mom had filled him in that a guest named Sophie was a paramedic who'd helped Jim, it didn't take much to put two-and-two together. He didn't have much experience with medical stuff, but he knew that job had to be difficult and demanding at times.

"How long have you been a paramedic?" Small talk was mostly a foreign concept, but he forced it because it kept his dick under control at the moment. Sophie turned and walked across the bridge to the opposite rail and looked down.

"I had six years in." There was terseness in her tone that warned him not to dig any deeper, but it just made him all the more curious. If something had happened to her job, it would probably explain her moods.

"Had?" He pressed with a queasy sensation in his gut. God, he *was* making small talk. Sophie rubbed her arms with her hands and gave a little shrug. "Yeah, well, I'm in between jobs right now." Well there, he'd just solved the puzzle. Case, and the need for small talk, closed. Sophie's sandals softly padded over the worn plank floor as she strolled to the mouth of the bridge and turned back to him with a crooked smile.

"Look, it's a Montana time machine." She stepped completely out of the bridge. "Modern day." Then she stepped back inside. "Back in time. It's like someone stole time, stuffed it inside here, and everything just…stood still."

Tucker couldn't argue with that. Most of the bridge was original, down to the square-headed iron nails and hand-hewn log support beams. There was something about looking up and seeing the exposed crisscross roof supports and the faded red paint that wrapped you in old arms and squeezed. He got what she was saying and it surprised him. He'd never met anyone else who shared quite that same sensation. Sophie strolled back toward him to the increased tempo of rain.

"Wouldn't it be great to steal time? I'd steal July…take the whole damn month and force it to slow down. To stop. Then things wouldn't…happen so fast." Her words weren't really meant for him. He didn't reply, just watched her with a growing knot in his gut as she wandered closer. Her words might not be for him, but the look in her eyes sure as hell was.

For a pretty little thing, she sure had something heavy ripping her up inside. He knew that look on her face — sadness over something you can't control and longing for something you can't have. Heavy shadow wrapped them up as the storm increased. A wet, warm breeze kissed his cheek and ruffled Sophie's hair as she came closer until she stood, arms crossed, just a breath from him.

"Can't really stop time, huh?"

Tucker chucked her under the chin when she looked up at him. "No. But you can fill the time you do have and make it good." He snagged her elbow, pulled her closer. Sophie uncrossed her arms and turned, resting her butt against the railing as rain fell into the river in the open space behind her. Yeah, he might not be good enough for a sweet woman like Sophie, but as long as she offered a little sugar, there couldn't be any harm in taking a little taste.

Her head tipped back, her bottom lip turning inward just a bit beneath the top teeth. "Good would be your lips on me, Tucker Haywood."

She didn't have to ask twice. Tucker scooped her neck in his hand and pulled her in, bending down in one easy movement. She stepped into him, one arm going around his back, the other hand braced on his chin like they were meant to fit this way. It was so easy, how they moved and connected and reached for each other. He didn't allow himself to think on that as he pressed her body against the railing.

Sophie dove into his mouth with a mixture of languid and frenzied kisses. He let her lead, absorbing every soft and hard press of her lips, relishing the taste of her tongue and the deep heat of her mouth. His hat went flying, the top snaps of his shirt popping one by one. When she'd bared his chest halfway, Sophie dipped her lips to his neck, tracing a wet trail over his vein. Tucker closed his eyes, forgetting for a second that he didn't allow women to touch him like this. He pulled her mouth away to claim it with his own before sliding her shirt up to lift the fabric off her body. She untied the bikini top, her mouth finding his neck again for another round of slow torture. She held the bikini in place with her arm, teasing him.

"Hey now," he growled, feeling her smile against his skin. Sharp little tingles, like cold razors, bristled along the length of his collarbone, and down his chest. Sophie could take control so easily. Leaving him vulnerable and wanting, but there was no way in hell he'd allow himself to be at her mercy. He'd been at a woman's mercy once in his lifetime and the pain that had resulted was enough for a lifetime. He unfastened her shorts, yanked them down along with her panties.

"Tucker," she gushed.

"Do you want to stop?" He grabbed her hips.

"No. I was going to tell you to go faster." She moved her arm and the bikini top fell away. Tucker swore, lifted her onto the rail. She grabbed his shoulders in a death grip. Before she could protest at being so close to a ten-foot drop, he spread her arms out and placed her hands on the support beams beside her. As soon as she gripped the beams, he sucked a nipple into his mouth. Her head went back with a moan. One arm looped securely around her hips. He unfastened his belt and jeans with the other. Glad he'd had lots of practice undressing one-handed. It was suddenly very, very worth it.

"I've got you, Soph. You won't fall." He moved a hand between her thighs. She parted them quickly, her hips jerking forward. Tucker rested his fingers on the inside of her leg; drawing gentle back and forth motions over her sensitive thigh.

"Maybe I want to fall," she whispered as she arched a little, seeking the touch he kept just out of reach. He couldn't deny her. Tucker parted her swiftly, tracing a finger over her clit. She jerked with a cry; he grabbed her waist more firmly to keep her from falling, pressing harder, faster, against her willing nub. He wanted to pull her off the railing and move her to the floor, spread her out and taste all of her. Sophie's head was thrown back, her hair streaming down into nothingness between her and the water below, her breasts round and full and Tucker knew this was perfect. Just the way it was meant to be.

He held his breath for several beats, listening to Sophie's soft pants and moans mix with the ripple of water and the pound of rain. The sounds filled him with an unnerving peace, which he shoved away so pure lust could take hold. He brought her up for a deep, open kiss, flicking his finger in the way that made her gasp the most. Her thighs clenched, her middle going rigid as moisture cascaded around his hand and she screamed into his mouth.

"Jesus, Sophie!" He moved back a bit, positioned her hips on the very edge of the rail.

"Condom!" her voice was so breathy, it took a minute to register. Shit. He groaned against her neck in frustration, kneading her hips with his fingers. He didn't make a point of carrying that particular item around with him during the workday. There was a time when he might have had one in the truck, but his prowling days were mostly over. Or had been, until he'd met her.

"Don't have one." The waver of defeat in his voice made Tucker cringe. Her breaths were long and unsteady. Whispers of rain breezed in against his face.

"I'm on the pill," Sophie blinked as if she were trying to clear her vision. "I'm otherwise safe and if you tell me you are too, I'll believe you. But if you're not sure, then…" Tucker moved his hands up to her waist and back down, reluctant to lose this contact with her. He hadn't gone bareback since his fiancé had left him years ago, and he'd had an exam since then. Despite confidence in himself, her confidence in him made his chest clench.

"I am. And I'm sure if you are."

She reached down, grabbing his cock, guiding him into perfect position and signaling her answer. Tucker let lose, driving into her with one violent thrust. Her cry urged him on, encouraged him to take her however he wanted. Rough. Hard. The way she craved him. An overwhelming sense of incompletion raged through him. He thrust harder, pulling her tighter against him and it still wasn't enough. The tight, hot slide of her body milked nuances and intense sensations he couldn't recall ever feeling, but it wasn't enough. He wanted to be farther, deeper.

He wanted to be closer.

Sophie's upper body leaned back over the rail. "Don't stop!" she cried, arching into his hard thrusts with an expression of pure abandon on her face. He flicked her tender clit and she cried his name with a fractured sound. And that was enough; that was the completion he craved as he spilled into her, grinding his face into her chest and holding her for all he was worth.

Breathing. There was nothing but the sound of their hard, unsteady breathing and the rippling water. Sophie lowered her arms and wrapped them, trembling, around his neck so he could help her down. She didn't let go, just swayed against him with her forehead against his chest.

Tucker reached for her hair, hesitated just a moment before running his palm over the back of her head. This was intimate, too intimate and unfamiliar. Sex was a quick affair, one that led to a quick departure. Not feelings like those crashing around in his chest right now. Certainly not the want to do it again, slowly, to learn what made her buck and scream, what touched her heart. He'd been down that road once already and it led to a drop off of daggers and self-doubt he couldn't erase.

Handing Sophie her shorts, Tucker turned away to give himself some distance as he righted his jeans. Then she touched his arm and they walked back to the truck in a post-sex glow that wrapped around him like heat from a winter fire. He slid into the truck and so did she, and then, God help him, she lay down on the seat with her head on his lap and for once, Tucker had no idea what to do next.

• • •

There was no way he was staying in the ranch house tonight. Not after the glory that was Sophie had him in a slow, hot burn. With his mom gone visiting family in Missoula for the night, he'd be alone in the house and it would be aggravatingly quiet and…lonely. He'd dropped Sophie off at the cabin and got himself out to check pastures. Her hot, sweet body followed him every second and now, cloaked in dark and exhausted from finding menial things to keep himself busy, Tucker was edgy as hell. If he couldn't have Sophie, he at least needed someone to take his mind off her. Another warm body to fill the space, to remind him he wasn't alone.

He grabbed fresh clothes from the ranch house and strolled down to the row-style bunkhouse the onsite hands lived in. He pounded on Jaxon's door. A few seconds and muffled curses later, Jax cracked the door with sleepy eyes.

"What?"

"Let me in."

Jaxon swung the door wide, rubbing his eyes with one hand. He wasn't one to turn down the chance to fall asleep early, and while nine at night didn't suit Tucker well for crashing for the night, Jaxon had no qualms.

"You sick?" Jax yawned.

"Nope."

"Drunk?"

Tucker grunted. "I wish, but no." He kicked off his boots at the door and crossed the room to the sofa. Jaxon had the largest unit with two rooms and a private bathroom. Bunking down with Jaxon wasn't new. There was a time when he, Cole, and Levi spent more time sleeping on Jax's floor than they did in their own beds. When Jaxon came to Paint River as a kid, he'd had a room in the ranch house, but quickly decided living under the same roof as Tucker's father, Cooper, wasn't for him. He'd moved to the bunkhouse with the other men with a small sleeping area and a communal bathroom and kitchen. By sixteen, he had won the private quarters on a bet. A very painful bet, one Tucker bore the scars of.

His brain shifted to Sophie's finger tracing the brand on his back. Tank McGee, one of their oldest and longest running hands at the time, had the private bunk, had for years. When Jaxon said he wanted it, Tank challenged him. Get branded, get the private bunk. No one imagined a teenager would put himself through that kind of pain for a bedroom with a small living space and private bathroom. Jax whipped his shirt off that instant. Both terrified, and proud of his friend's determination, Tucker offered himself up too so Jax wouldn't have to do it alone.

That searing hot brand pressing into his skin was the most physically painful experience of his life.

The bunkhouse had turned into the perfect escape for the Haywood boys when their father got to be too much to tolerate. Maeve used to shoo them out of the ranch house, knowing full well where they were going, and reassuring them she could handle their father. Her method of handling Cooper was to remain a quiet shadow until he'd raged himself into exhaustion. Despite her reassurances, Tucker had never been comfortable leaving her, but as a young boy, he'd felt helpless to stand up for her against his dad.

When he'd gotten older, stronger, bigger than Cooper, Tucker had made a habit of putting himself between his parents like a brick wall—keeping Maeve out of Cooper's tornado, and taking the brunt of the storm himself. They'd all stopped coming to the bunkhouse with Jaxon then, and it had been years since Tucker had stayed the night here.

He brushed off the memories and had no sooner thrown himself on the sofa than Jaxon was asleep again in the adjoining bedroom. He lay there, listening to his friend's soft snores, staring at the shadows the table lamp cast on the ceiling. This place was home as much as the big house on the hill. As he settled in, he thought of Sophie. Jaxon's rumbling echoed behind Tucker's thoughts of soft blue eyes and a full pink mouth as he sunk into sleep, and it felt just right.

Chapter Ten

Learning ballet was a balance of foundation steps, those that supported everything else learned later. Forget the early basics and sometimes the more advanced footwork and movements would fail. Sophie figured breathing was a little like ballet. Her mother's body, once graceful and strong with the basic movements of life, now struggled to remember the early steps, causing everything else to stumble. Her lungs were healthy. They could hold all the air her body needed, if only her brain could send the correct signals to put breathing back into a normal rhythm instead of the shallow, stunted effort it had become.

Her brain wasn't sending anything correctly anymore. Sometimes Violet's breathing stopped completely, only to resume with gasping breaths. Her pulse raced, then it slowed down, and then raced again. No matter how much she struggled to maintain life, there was nothing anyone could do to make it easier to live, or to die. Violet, as she had always done, would complete her life in her own way. Sophie tried to remember that as she watched the rise and fall of Violet's thin chest beneath the pink blanket.

Even though Sophie had been coming to visit several times a year for the past two years, it still seemed that she hadn't had nearly enough time with her mother. Sophie looked down at her knotted fingers as guilt flooded her. She'd never admit it to Carla; had a hard enough time admitting it to herself, but each time she'd visited Violet in the nursing home, Sophie left with the determination that she wasn't going to visit her mother again. It was too hard to see Violet withering away, too difficult to deal with the loss of her mother's vitality. It was one thing when an ambulance patient teetered on death's door, but to have her own flesh and blood shuffling toward that precipice was unbearable. Yet, each time she told herself she couldn't visit Violet again, Sophie knew that she would. Because she couldn't not come. She still needed her mother so much.

If Violet were healthy, they would have a normal mother-daughter conversation in which Sophie spilled her guts about losing her job, and running out of money; about Tucker. She'd confess that she felt like a failure, that her life was so far off-track, she couldn't find her way back on. Knowing Violet, she'd pat Sophie's hand and tell her to put on big girl panties and deal with it, sister. It's life. You'll know what to do when the time comes—her favorite piece of advice to dish out.

Sophie held back tears. Maybe she'd even ask her mom how to make peach pie, just in case she needed a secret Tucker weapon. There'd been a time when Violet had made all the delicious things, filling their small apartment with the stomach-fluttering scent of baked goods. All that homemade yumminess had fallen off the radar as Sophie and Carla grew. A mother with three jobs and two non-stop, expensive-to-raise daughters didn't leave much time for embracing the inner Martha Stewart.

What she needed more than a pie lesson was a warm

shoulder to lean on and a feminine hand with beautiful, oval tipped nails to stroke her cheek and tell her life would be fine. She needed the scent of Red Door perfume and the throaty laugh that never hesitated to grace Sophie's ears.

She just needed her mom.

Taking Violet's hand, Sophie studied her mother's face. Her time with Tucker on the bridge had been amazing. It was just the kind of thing she'd share with Violet, minus the sex, of course, though her mom would know without being told. She'd tell her about the amazing beauty of the land, but she wouldn't tell her how much that beauty hurt to see. Because it did. Sophie never imagined herself a country girl, but the landscape took her breath away and filled her up with a sense of awe. Yet, each time she got lost in the distant mountains or the stretches of fields dotted with colorful flowers, bitterness rose up. It was hard to connect with the beauty around her when it reminded her so much of her mother's struggle. Montana wasn't just Violet's last vacation spot. It was her prison.

Sophie smoothed her mother's hair back and placed a kiss on her forehead. For the first time, she was glad she didn't have a job to run back to, one that would dictate how long she got to spend here before she had to return. She'd be able to stay with Violet this time, as long as she wanted to. The dwindling clock in her mother's lifespan might decide to add a few more hours, or hit snooze at any moment. There was no way to tell, but if Sophie was able to rearrange things a bit, she could be available to be here, to be present, with her mom until the end.

She could get a job right here in Missoula, maybe find a place to stay for a while and see how it went instead of returning to Minnesota and continuing her job search there. Stay here. In Montana. Closer to her mom, her sister, for all that was worth...and to Tucker. It all depended on if she was hired for the hospital job she'd interviewed for back in Minnesota, she supposed. Until then, it didn't hurt to make other plans.

"What do you think about that, mom?" she found herself saying, as if she'd shared her thoughts out loud. Violet wasn't able to respond to what people said to her, but it didn't mean she didn't hear or understand them. Sophie knew this, but it always seemed strange to talk to Violet when she knew she wouldn't get a response—like talking to a doll instead of a living person. Her mom loved this land. Maybe Montana didn't have to be a prison if Sophie could continue to paint images of the beauty Violet had loved so much. No harm could come of giving Violet a verbal photo album. Maybe it would be a little healing for them both.

"I bet you didn't know there's a covered bridge about an hour away from here, mom," Sophie began softly. "I met someone, a cowboy. Seriously, like a real cowboy with a hat and a really big horse…"

• • •

"What's that?" Jaxon eyed Tucker suspiciously.

Tucker sniffed, took a big bite. "Cookie."

"Your ma make those?" Jaxon edged closer, looping rope. Tucker watched him with amusement, taking another bite for effect. The shit-eating twinkle in Jaxon's eyes meant no good was about to go down. Yeah, they were juveniles where baked goods were concerned. He wasn't too macho to admit he had a hell of a sweet tooth and wasn't afraid to feed it.

"Yup." He chewed, gave his friend a wink. "They're good, too."

Jax hung the looped rope over a fence post, held out one dusty gloved hand. "Knowing you, you've got a whole pocket full."

"You know I don't share." Before he could reach for the stash of cookies in his shirt pocket, Jaxon railed him against the fence. Tucker laughed, swiveling to one side, but not quick enough to avoid Jax's big arm banding around his chest. Tucker grabbed Jax's wrist with one hand, reached behind him and grabbed a fistful of shirt with the other. With a grunt, he tossed Jax cattywampus over his shoulder. Both men spun, Jaxon's back slamming into the gate.

Jaxon's smile was amused and easy. They'd been squaring off for years. Jaxon was the only man on the ranch to match Tucker's size, and both of them loved the chance to get the better of the other. Thirty-one was not too old for a good old-fashioned smack-down. Pinning his friend with an elbow in his chest, Tucker reached into his pocket and pulled out a cookie. He wagged it in front of Jaxon's hungry eyes.

"This one is yours." He ate it, shrugged with a snort. "Oops." Jaxon grabbed Tucker's shirt with both hands, shoved him back. A dog skittered past, nearly getting trampled by Tuck's boots. They locked arms, faced off, breathing hard.

"I've known you a long time, Tuck, " Jaxon snickered, getting the advantage and spinning Tucker around in a dance of twisted arms and tangled feet. "So far, I've only seen two things bring you to your knees: the blonde in cabin eighteen with the little yellow bikini, and your ma's double chocolate chip."

Tucker arched his back, his neck tingling at the mention of Sophie. It was just enough distraction to give the other man full advantage. He pinned Tucker's arms behind his back, kicked his knees out with one boot and laughed as Tucker's legs buckled and he fell to his knees. Jaxon reached over Tucker's shoulder and nabbed the rest of the cookies from his pocket.

"Make that three, since I totally just whooped your ass."

Tucker jumped up as fast as he went down, making a swipe for the cookies Jaxon was shoving in his mouth. "Sophie has not brought me to my knees," he scoffed. "She's…entertainment." The words sounded wrong as they left his lips. Sophie was entertaining, for sure, but cheapening their intimacy made Tucker want to punch himself. His subconscious had tried to wiggle in some complex thought over his exact feelings for one Sophie Miller, but Tucker had shut it down each time. No sense in wasting time or energy on hemming-and-hawing over possibilities he'd never actually pursue.

"Like hell. You don't *entertain* the same woman twice."

"Jaxon," Tucker warned, knowing the look in his friend's eye all too well. When his friend wanted something, he wanted it now. In that, they were a lot alike. Impatient, greedy, and when it came down to it, a little selfish. They both had a Cooper Haywood streak in them, though Tucker was the only one who had inherited it by blood. They'd both learned by example though, it seemed.

"You blew off haying over at Agate Falls to take her to the bridge." Jaxon slid him a knowing look. "When have you ever dumped work for a woman? Never. So, it's about time you tell me what's going on with this girl, 'cause I'm tired of waiting for you to come out with it already."

Tucker's spine tingled. His face scrunched as he tried to recall when he'd missed haying at the neighboring ranch. Then it hit him, that's what he'd forgotten the morning he got caught up in Sophie and taken his good old time loving her up on the bridge. He'd gotten invested in her and, in turn, forgotten about his responsibilities. The ranch needed a steady hand to keep it going, and that meant him while Cole was away. Even if his brother had been here, Tucker would have a hard time forgiving himself for skipping out on work.

Anger flashed hot and quick. "God damn it!"

Jaxon gave a don't-worry-about-it smile. "It was just hay. And it rained, so we quit early anyway." Jaxon leaned toward Tucker. "So…is she finally *the one*?"

"You obviously have a death wish, Jax." Tucker slammed his hands into his leather gloves and beat the dust off his jeans. The Independence Day heat was seeping through every layer of clothing, making him sweaty and impatient. To be honest, he was feeling downright mean at the moment. Enough talking about Sophie—thinking about her. But Jaxon had a thick skull to match his muscles, apparently.

"What? It's a legitimate question."

"Been there, done that. There will never be a *one*." He adjusted the strap of his chaps over his right hip, fiddling with the buckle longer than he needed to. "It's time for you to shut the fuck up."

Jax went on like a stupid man. "I know you like to tell yourself that." He slapped Tucker on the shoulder with a glove. "Just because you chose not to fight for Jewel doesn't mean you won't have a chance with someone else, Tuck. It's time to move on; see what happens. In the meantime, I'll sit back, munching on your mama's cookies, and watch the show."

Tucker flinched inwardly at the mention of Jewel's name. No, he hadn't fought for her when her father backed him into a wall and said no son of Cooper Haywood's would ever be good enough. He hadn't given in to her pleas to elope because he wasn't the kind of man who'd steal a girl away from her family like that. Despite his money and ranching success, it all boiled down to being the son of a mean-spirited womanizer who'd made a sour name for himself in this small community and tarnished his sons by proxy. And for all his temper and inability to stick to one woman, Tucker wasn't far behind. It's what people assumed about him after all, so why bother to change perception, right? He was who he was and he had better things to do with his time than to try and convince people he was a good guy.

Besides, how many bad relationship examples did one guy need? His parent's marriage had been rocky at best; his brother Cole's first wife, Livy, had used him for his money and run off with a chunk of it, leaving their daughter, Birdie behind. Combined with the Jewel-experience, Tucker had his fill of love gone wrong. When Jaxon opened his mouth again, Tucker clenched his jaw.

Jaxon put his palms out and took a teasing step back. "I'm shutting up now."

"You're lucky you're like a brother to me, asshole." Despite his attempt at lightheartedness, Tucker figured he was in a bit of trouble. He might not be able to recall the sweeter details of his first love, but the passion he felt for Sophie was screaming loud and clear. She only had a few days left here at Paint River, and then she'd be moving on. Probably wouldn't hurt to set her straight anyway, about this thing between them. It wasn't going to go anywhere. He was fine with that, and though Sophie hadn't given him any indication that she was going to turn into the clingy, let's-make-this-more type, it was better to be safe than sorry.

He should clear it up for her, just in case. Tonight. Yeah, but he liked having her here, oddly. Every time he'd seen a squirrel these past couple of days, he'd busted up. City girl with a spatula—her shirt falling off one shoulder, tight thighs peeking beneath the hem of worn, denim shorts. His lips twitched with the remembered feel of her mouth on his and the fucking hot sounds that had come from her throat when he'd spread her out on the bridge.

This had to quit. Shaking it off, Tucker nodded toward the horse Jaxon had tied to the fence.

"You ready to saddle up so we can get going?" Enough chatter, enough Sophie. They had fences to check the rest of the afternoon before the annual Fourth of July party at the neighboring ranch, Agate Falls, tonight. Tucker hadn't planned on attending, but now that he had to apologize to Agate Falls' owner Darren Waite for missing the haying party the other day, he was obligated.

He left Jax to go into the barn to retrieve his own gelding. Usually empty this time of day, Tucker was surprised to hear a feminine giggle, followed by a man's deep, intimate laugh, waft down the center aisle. He paused, eyes searching the refracted light, certain he was about to walk in on a ranch hand and one of the kitchen staff or something. It wouldn't be the first time.

The laughing got closer as he approached his horses' stall. He coughed loudly behind a smile to prevent any awkwardness, and possibly give the gigglers time to get their clothes back on. Movement from the stall next to the one he was going toward made him pause again. Two heads peeked out of the stall door. Tucker's stomach bottomed out as he did a double-take of the pair of flushed faces and kiss-puffy lips.

"Oh my god, Ma?"

Maeve slid sheepishly out of the stall, Jim Gilfoyle following behind, holding her hand. She looked as embarrassed as Tucker felt, but Jim, he just looked proud of himself. Maeve held the top of her button-down shirt together with her free hand. "Tucker! I thought you'd already left."

Tucker grimaced and looked away. He'd just busted his mother, in the barn, making out with…hell, with Jim. He had to have seen this coming, because, really, Jim had stayed on at the ranch for almost an entire year straight. In all the years Tucker could remember Jim coming to stay at the ranch for his yearly writing retreat, the mystery author always returned to Chicago eventually. More like an uncle than just a family friend, he had always doted on the boys, bringing them gifts, writing, calling, and celebrating their accomplishments. Considering his mother had known Jim since she was a child, and they'd stayed in touch all these years through marriages and children, this…well, this was a natural progression.

"Tucker," Maeve began, but he stopped her with a wave of his hand.

"I just need my horse, Ma. Pretend I'm not here." *No, no.* "Scratch that. Just wait to pick up where you left off *after* I get my horse." He moved fast to the stall, unlocked it, and, without bothering to put a halter on his gelding, clicked his tongue. Like a well-trained dog, the horse followed him without a lead rope.

He tried not to look at his mother because he didn't want to see that love-tussled look on her face, but, dang, he did look, and there it was. Her smile was placating, but he didn't need to be reassured or calmed down. He wasn't upset…not really. Why shouldn't she move on with her life? His father had been dead almost three years. Her marriage to him had been more obligation than love. Cooper didn't dish out affection. He had only taken what he wanted and pounded obedience out of his family the same way he had manipulated the land, working long hours to the point where his family could go weeks with barely a glimpse of him. As much as he despised the hard man Cooper was, every now and then, Tucker mourned the reality that he'd never had someone to show him what being a family man was really about.

He tried to walk past them, but Maeve shot to his side and put a gentle grip on his shoulder. The sad twist of her expression spoke volumes to him. He'd always been able to read his mother like an open book, even when she worked so hard to hold her feelings inside. She was worried about what he thought. At the moment, Tucker didn't know. Really, was it his place to even have an opinion? If she wanted to erase the memories of a loveless marriage with a man who brought her happiness, then who was he to stop her?

Even if he'd never have that same measure of happiness for himself. He didn't know how to handle a relationship, and why set himself up with a wife who might someday come to resent him, the way they'd all resented his father? He was pretty set in that way of thinking, so the pang of envy he got just then was way out of left field.

Tucker blinked hard and cupped his mother's cheek with his palm. "It's okay, Ma." Without waiting for her response, he led his horse out. Let Maeve scrub her slate clean. It just reinforced Tucker's belief that having a slate in the first place was a really bad idea.

· · ·

Night had fallen by the time Sophie returned to Paint River Ranch from the nursing home. Emotionally spent, she let herself in the cabin and collapsed face down on the sofa. Her feet hung over the end, her hair strewn around her shoulders. The cushion pressed into her face, threatening suffocation, but she managed to pull thready mouthfuls of air. It was an uncomfortable position, but she was too tired to care.

She'd spent almost four hours with her mother, talking to her off and on as if a real, two-sided conversation would miraculously begin at any moment. After a while, it didn't matter anymore that Violet wasn't responding vocally. She'd responded in other ways, Sophie was sure. Maybe she was nuts, but there were a few times when her mother's eyes opened at just the right time, or she rolled her head to the side as if in agreement with something Sophie had said. She and Violet used to talk for hours, and even once she'd left home for her own apartment, Sophie had called her mom every day. Every damn day. When she'd said good-bye a little over two years ago, as Violet left for a two-week vacation to visit Carla here in Missoula, Sophie never imagined the epic conversation they'd had before Violet had left would be the last of its kind for them. And yet, today, simply talking to her as if nothing had changed had been uplifting. And sensing that Violet was responding in her own way? There just weren't words for how awesome that was.

Sophie had actually been whistling when she'd walked out of the nursing home. Until her patched-together, but mostly-still-broken cell phone gave an angry squeal to announce a new voicemail. One that told her she hadn't gotten the unit coordinator position back in Minnesota. Their decision to hire "in house" meant she was firmly down to the last set of twenties in her wallet, with no financial-boosting reason to go home at the moment.

Seriously, life's ups and downs could kiss her ass.

"Trying to let in more squirrels?"

Sophie jerked at the voice, cranking her head too fast and rolling onto the floor. So much for staying put. Tucker's half smile blossomed into a full on I'm-completely-laughing-at-you grin. Her body responded immediately as if he'd given her some hidden command with that smile. *Nipples, perk up!* She considered covering her chest with an arm to hide the evidence, but Tucker held out a hand to help her up. "You left the door open again." Too surprised to be completely embarrassed, she took it.

"I did?"

"Yep." He paused and looked her over. "Go get ready." Sophie glanced down at her wrinkled capri pants and V-neck tee. She had no idea what he was talking about.

"Go?"

He pointed to the sky and mimicked an explosion with his fingers. "It's the Fourth of July, silly. There's a party and fireworks at the ranch down the road. Unless," he ran the backs of his fingers down her bare arms. "You're in the mood to keep the fireworks inside."

She warmed at his touch, her breasts actually aching this time, but the sluggishness of emotional fatigue made it difficult to enjoy. Sophie crossed her arms, attempting a smile but failing miserably. She didn't want to turn him down, because, really, she liked his company. And as up in the air as her life was, there was a good possibility that she wouldn't get much more of it. Still, her social gene had the consistency of a wet pancake at the moment.

"I don't want to go anywhere, Tucker. But thank you."

He shrugged. "Well, I want you to, so get ready."

Sophie crossed her arms with an incredulous huff. Her heart thumped a little faster as her inner feminist wondered when arrogant had become so sexy. "All about you, huh?"

He slid his hat off and set it on the arm of the couch before turning back to her. His hands slowly, gently smoothed up her forearms, nudging her crossed arms apart. Sophie's breath caught in that hard, out-of-control way. He took her chin in one hand and tipped her up with a wink.

"Oh, I think there was plenty of focus on what you wanted on the bridge, don't you think?" A needy ache shot between her legs, replaying the insistent need she'd given into, again, when he'd had her up against the bridge railing, with her upper body inches away from freefall. She'd fallen all right, straight into orgasm central, and she wanted another one right now.

God, what he did to her. Sophie squeezed her lids shut and tried to turn away from his grip. When he only held her tighter, she met his gaze with a challenge. Discomfort washed over his strong features. He regarded her for several long seconds, his lips parting once as if he was going to ask her what was wrong. Not that she would tell him. But he didn't ask, just let her go and took a step back.

Sophie didn't know what was more intense, his eyes or his biceps. A black T-shirt hugged his chest, showing off deep masculinity underneath. He smelled incredible, soapy and fresh with an underlying note of spice that wrapped around her and squeezed hard. Her resolve began to melt away. Tucker was so much more appealing than wallowing and, Jesus, if she could get him somewhere private for just one more mind-blowing ride, she would.

"I'll wait." His voice was low and a little edgy, as if he was completely out of his comfort zone. "While you change." He shifted from one boot to the other, his eyes sliding to the door. Muscle moved gracefully under the tanned skin of his forearms as he crossed them, his long fingers curling lightly into fists. Suddenly curious, she stepped before him and nudged his arms apart. Tucker hitched a brow as she took one of his hands and laid it over her palm.

Grasping the knuckle of his first finger between her thumb and middle finger, she ran her fingers lightly down the length. Rough skin met her touch and she flipped his hand, swirling one finger over the work-hardened calluses at the end of each fingertip and along the underside of his knuckles. Tucker's arm contracted forcefully, as if torn between pulling away and staying put. His fingers flexed under her ministrations and Sophie heard his breath stall.

"You have beautiful hands," Sophie whispered. The square palms and long, sturdy fingers were strong and capable. Secure. The hands of a man dedicated enough to do the work required. One who didn't stop until the job was done. Reliable. Like the man. They could touch with extreme pleasure or cause bruising pain. They could hold tightly—her hand, her heart.

With a quick intake of breath, Sophie let his hand drop. "Fine. I'll be right out." She crossed around the sofa to her room, shutting the bedroom door as if she could keep out the maelstrom of unwelcome tenderness she had for him just then. It followed her anyway.

Chapter Eleven

Sophie's first surprise was the 1964 Chevrolet Apache truck sitting outside her cabin. She didn't know squat about vehicles, but anyone would have been able to tell that the truck was ripped right out of the past and someone had taken a lot of time to make it pretty again. She took in the angular design, flawless navy blue paint, and gleaming wooden truck bed before peeking in on smooth two-tone gray leather seats.

"Meet Daisy." Tucker gave a grand sweep of his arms. "This is Levi's baby." She listened as he told her about his brother Levi, the Marines, and Afghanistan, while she walked around the truck and appreciated its beauty. "We started working on this thing years ago, before we were even old enough to drive." He looked over the hood, staring off into the night. "Gave us something to do besides work cattle and listen to Da—" Tucker cleared his throat and pushed away from the truck, coming around to open the door for her. Sophie gave an interested smile, hoping he'd finish whatever he'd stopped himself from saying, but he didn't.

She slid inside and ran her hands over the glossy wooden

dash. "Daisy, huh? She's beautiful."

Tucker got in and turned the key. The truck started with a huge rumble. "I take it out now and then, keep her running good. Considering I told Levi when we talked last night that I hit a deer with it and smashed the front end to bits, let's hope nothing bad really does happen." He winked and pulled out of the yard.

"Why in the world would you tell your brother that you smashed his truck?" Teasing a soldier stuck in Afghanistan seemed a little heartless. And apparently, by the look of childish glee on Tucker's face, was the type of thing the Haywood brothers did.

"Because it's fun." The yard lights faded into the distance, swathing them in night. "And it'll make him think about repeatedly kicking my ass when he does get home, which can take his mind off other things." Sophie gave him a look that displayed she wasn't convinced. Tucker rolled his eyes. "I just had it painted. I'm going to take a pic and surprise him when we Skype next week."

He dug something from the center console and held it up. "We found this penny inside the glove compartment when we bought the truck. About a week after we got Daisy, Levi took her out in the field without Ma or Dad knowing, hit a rut, and rolled her." The penny caught in the light as Tucker flipped it in his palm. "We found him lying in the grass with this damn penny sitting right in the middle of his chest. He was fine and ever since, this has been his lucky charm." Tucker probably had no idea how wistful and full of longing his voice was. Sophie found herself clinging to every word and every nuance of inner Tucker that was peeking at her.

"He gave this penny away once, and it came right back. It showed up, right here in the center console…just like it had been waiting for him to come home. It's silly, but every time I get in this seat, I look to make sure it's still there."

Sophie blinked as her eyes began to burn, another blink releasing one tear down her cheek. She startled at the warmth and quickly wiped it away, hoping he didn't see. Then again, so what if he did? There was a lot of love inside that big man and he was oblivious to the fact that it was even there, she bet.

"He's lucky to have you," she whispered. He looked down and gave a short laugh, shrugging as if trying to dislodge her words. The space inside her chest squeezed, some primal instinct trying to force her into embracing him. But Sophie held back. Tucker didn't seem the kind to want or need comfort when his emotions were tumbling—no, the stiffness of his spine and hard set to his lips displayed this conversation had already gone further than he was comfortable with.

She cleared her throat and shifted a little in the seat. "Ready?" Her cheery voice broke the tension and brought the gleam back to his eyes, leaving Sophie with the sensation she'd just encountered a very rare emotional moment.

Her second surprise was the amount of people congregated in the yard at Agate Falls ranch. Tucker had explained on the drive over that Agate Falls was strictly a working cattle ranch. Owned by Darren Waite, his daughter, and two sons, the ranch neighbored Paint River and the properties shared pasture land, equipment and, when needed, man power. Tucker's familiarity with Agate Falls was apparent as he parked behind a huge barn and led her through the crowd, stopping every second to chat with someone.

He made introductions Sophie had no chance in hell of ever remembering. A huge bonfire burned in the pasture behind the barn. Buckets and hay bales made a wide haphazard circle of seats around the fire. A BBQ pit offered five huge barrel grills and, to Sophie's shock, two fire spits with full body, split pigs roasting over open flame.

After a good twenty minutes of mingling, they made their way inside the barn. The doors were open on both ends, letting a warm breeze billow through. Multiple strings of tiny white lights were looped through the beams and ran the length of the barn. Round paper lanterns hung low from long wire, creating a cozy golden glow. Music bounced in the air high above the sound of laughter and conversation. Three men stood on a small platform on the south side of the barn erected from pallets.

The music stopped, the crowd grew louder. Tucker nudged her and pointed to a tall, mocha-skinned cowboy standing in the middle of a small, makeshift stage. She recognized him from the day he and Tucker had ridden to her cabin when the cows had gotten lose. He was holding a fiddle, flanked by two other men, one with a banjo and the other a guitar.

"My buddy Jaxon. He and my brother Cole are amazing fiddlers."

Jaxon stepped to the edge of the platform, raised the fiddle to his shoulder and burst into a commanding singsong. "In constant sorrow!" A huge pause in the conversation around them made Sophie's ears rush. And then a well of music rose up, and the crowd went berserk as the pickers played out, "I Am a Man of Constant Sorrow."

Jaxon winked at her as he stepped up to the microphone, his hand claiming it like a prize as he drew it near and began belting out the blue grass lyrics. Around them, a wide circle of dancing couples formed, reminding Sophie of a two-stepping redneck party from the movies. She glanced around with equal parts amusement and surprise, realizing she'd never seen so many cowboy hats, jeans, denim skirts, and boots all in one place. She looked down at her spring green, organic hemp wrap dress and golden ballet flats. With her two-tone hair and dangling gold hoops, Sophie figured she'd stepped through the metro portal and straight into a country western landscape where the only redneck in the room was her.

Nothing screamed outsider like organic hemp in a barn full of leather boots.

"Do you dance?"

Sophie snapped up to Tucker's smiling face. "Dance?" She gave a furtive glance to the swirling bodies around them. "Ah, yes, actually I do. But…not this kind of dancing." She'd no sooner gotten the words out than Tucker had her by the hands and pulled her into the circle.

"Well, you've been missing out then," he said. "Because this is the only dancing that matters." He grabbed her hand while his other arm slipped around her back. She balked as he pulled her forward and took two quick steps back. And then she was pulled up against his chest and he twirled her around twice. They were swept up in the circle with no way out, and Sophie found it easy to follow Tucker's steps. Probably because he held her so tightly she'd become an extension of him and had no choice but to mimic his movements. And she wasn't complaining. One big hand was firm against her back, his fingers splayed, and every so often she'd bump against him. When she was very lucky, her pelvis would press against his thigh as they went 'round, briefly, but long enough to give her a flash of anticipation for his touch.

"Not bad for a city girl." He spun her around gently before clasping her back against his chest. The top buttons were done up on his shirt and she itched to let a few loose, give a lick to skin that she remembered tasted as good as he smelled.

Sophie gasped as he twirled her fast and tight. Her leg muscles were lose, her body pliable to the moves he was putting her through. It was good, so good, to be out here, dancing again. "Twenty years of dance. Eleven as a student and nine as an instructor."

He gave an impressed smile. "You don't happen to teach ballet, do you? My little niece Birdie has been begging Cole for ballet lessons for months."

"Yeah, actually, I do."

Tucker rolled his eyes. "Birdie is going to be all over you when she gets home from Australia in a few weeks. Her tutu collection is insane." His words were heavy with an affection that filled her with warmth at the love he had for one little girl. For a second, Sophie had a blip of excited nervousness at the idea of meeting Tucker's family. Until she remembered that she had no idea where she'd be in a few weeks. And the possibility that she and Tucker would be sharing any kind of time together? Highly, highly unlikely. The thought of going back to the metro gave her instant heartburn. The gloss of the city was in such huge contrast to the simplistic style of this barn with its slightly sagging crossbeams in the ceiling, and hay-strewn floor. There was nothing out here but field and mountains and animals and…quiet. In the few short days she'd been at Paint River, and now this ranch, Sophie realized one thing: it was comfortable here—almost more comfortable than the metro she grew up in, the metro that oddly felt a little less like home. Carla had made an off-handed comment that Montana sucked the old life out of you and put a new one back in. Sophie thought her sister might be on to something there.

"I loved teaching. It was the only thing keeping me sane most times." She stumbled, her elbow hitting the back of the man behind her. Sophie shot him an apologetic grimace, but the man only smiled and gave her a polite nod.

"Sane?" Tucker shook his head as she stepped on his foot.

"Working as a paramedic can get a little stressful. Dance was my out, I guess. How I neutralized." They passed in front of the trio. Jaxon loved being up on the microphone like he was born with it, his caramel skin glowing under the soft barn lights. The even tone of his perfect tenor entwined with the banjo and guitar notes like a lover with slow, easy hands. This wasn't her normal choice of music. She'd barely listened to anything remotely country-ish unless one of her paramedic partners changed the radio station in the ambulance and forced her to. This was catchy and soulful and gave Sophie an inane sense of peace and belonging. Considering how absorbed everyone else was in the music and dance, she figured she wasn't the only one to feel its spell.

"You don't teach anymore?"

Sophie looked at her feet, trying to follow Tucker's footsteps without stepping on him again. "I stopped when I was let go from the ambulance…" Her lips went numb as she stopped the words, glancing up to see if he was really listening. Explaining how her soul had gone so flat that she couldn't bring herself to try and teach the joy and beauty of dance to eager little children seemed too personal to share with a man she wasn't letting any deeper into her life. He seemed to be waiting for her to continue. Surprised by his obvious interest, and a little tempted to go on with her story, Sophie shook her head instead. "Yeah, I just…don't dance anymore."

"Mmmm." The rumble vibrated against her skin when Tucker pressed his jaw against her cheek. "Well I'm glad you decided to take it up again. Right now. With me."

His lips barely grazed her ear, leaving behind an electric zing as evidence that a small touch had occurred. Instantly, every inch of her skin became hypersensitive with the want to be touched, to seek it out, to demand it. She'd had lovers before, of course, but nowhere in her memory of the men who had touched her before could she recall an intensity of *need* or this raw, greedy anticipation that Tucker sparked in her. It was so easy to forget that anything existed beyond the moments when his hands were on her, his lips trailing over her skin.

Her chest rose and fell hard. Sophie focused on his touch

so intently that she didn't realize they'd stopped dancing. The beat of Tucker's chest matched her own, and the press of his hand against her back was harder. Sophie leaned into him so the tips of her breasts met his chest, her middle taking on his with a barely-there connection. Her hips longed to arch into him—begged for it—but she went rigid to keep her body under control. Because there were people around. A lot of people. Moving away from Tucker would be the best thing to do...just a step back, but instead, he moved closer yet, his lips again finding her ear. What control Sophie had on her breathing stopped when the heat of his mouth caressed her tender lobe. One brief touch—a fluttering contact that left her pulsing for more, was all that he gave her before pulling away.

"Did you like the bridge?" His low rumble vibrated through her body. She didn't need to dissect that question to know what he was asking.

"Yes."

The music ended to an exuberant round of clapping and cheering. His eyes were fixed on her as dancers began to filter off the dance floor. "Then follow me." He took her hand and led her outside where most of the crowd had gathered. Huge flames from the bonfire reached for the velvety, dark sky, but it had nothing on the heat in her blood at the moment. With only a few days left at Paint River Ranch, she supposed it didn't matter how she and Tucker spent their dwindling time together. The sex was amazing. Healing, almost in that it soothed her soul and helped her brain take a break from the constant stress. And Tucker—he just kept surprising her.

They crossed the yard and approached a stand of trees. Sophie looked up to the last clear patch of sky before branches took over. The inky stretch of night sky was dotted with brilliant stars that looked so close she could touch them. Big sky wasn't just a Montana moniker; it was an endearment that rubbed her soul like a crisp breath of fresh air.

Tucker finally pulled her along with a tug on her hand. "Watch this," he said, stepping onto a narrow path swallowed by the trees. Three steps in, lights on the ground blinked to life. Lining the path, the small white lights looked like they'd fallen from the sky. Sophie caught her breath.

"Come on." He linked their arms, pulling her close until she bumped into his side. "You'll love this, Fifi."

She followed him down the path, entranced by the lights, and swoony from Tucker's fresh, soapy scent and the feel of his solid arm under her hands. The path curved, dirt turning to stone beneath their feet. Sophie looked down to see large pavers leading to a staircase.

"What's this?"

"Look up." Tucker nudged her arm and pointed. The staircase led to a deck that lit up the same as the path had, the length of it winding around two huge trees, once, twice, leading upward to a structure nestled between the branches.

"Is that a…tree house?"

"Mmmhm." Tucker walked up the stairs to the deck. Taking her hand again, he led her up the staircase. The farther they went, the more lights came on. Sophie trailed her fingers around the bark of the trees as they walked, glancing up into the shadowy canopy partially blocked by the wide structure above. One last turn and they were at a sliding glass door and Sophie's middle clenched in sweet anticipation.

Tucker grabbed the door handle and more solar lights popped on, bathing them in a golden aura. He ushered her in ahead of him, closing the door softly as he entered. Crossing the room, Tucker grabbed battery-operated lanterns from the windowsill and flicked them on. The room was small, with a wicker loveseat and battered-looking wooden rocking chair in the middle of the room, arranged around a thick braided rug. A portion of tree trunk was visible and Sophie laughed when she saw that someone had used paint to create a fake fireplace, complete with orange flames, on the bark.

The tree house wasn't a shabby construction attempt. It was anything but. Smooth, shiny hardwood floors looked like they'd been professionally finished, four large windows carefully lined with trim. White molding edged the ceiling, rosettes meeting in each corner. It was a grown-up version of a childhood escape.

"Look up," Tucker said, pointing.

Above, a large clear panel offered an uninhibited view of the night sky. The branches above had either been cut away or parted just so, to let the sky in.

"Wow!" Sophie made a little circle, amazed that no matter which way she turned, she had a complete view of the night sky. Tucker wrapped his arms around her back and held her tight. Sophie trembled at the sweet, intimate way he held her. His lips dipped to her neck just below her ear. Her fingers tightened around his arms as Tucker nipped her neck, drawing out pings of pleasure with a sweet tug of pain. The contact opened a reserve of joy inside. One she'd long forgotten. In that moment, everything felt peaceful and calm and quiet inside her.

"Tucker," she started, but cut off with a hiss when one big hand slid the strap of her dress over her shoulder. Trying to pull out of the fog, Sophie twisted in his arms. "Tuck, wait."

He spun her against the fireplace-tree. Her hands went out against the bark in response. Before she could utter a syllable, Tucker's middle leaned into her ass and his hands were smoothing up her thighs, pushing her skirt up to her hips. He reached around and let the tie loose at her waist. The wrap dress parted, baring her front.

"Do you really want me to wait?" He nuzzled her hair out of the way with his face, trailing hot kisses over the back of her neck. Her body didn't want him to, but her heart did.

Sophie's palms pressed into the bark. "I want to know what we're doing."

Tucker grabbed her hips and drew her roughly against him. "I'm pretty sure you know what we're doing." His voice rumbled against her shoulder, his right hand smoothing around her middle and up to her breast. Before she could answer, his fingers slid beneath her bra and squeezed her nipple. Sophie bucked, dipping her head against the tree with a moan. He thrust his erection against her ass, palming her breast with another sharp pinch. Tucker was a maelstrom of touching, pulsing sensation, and Sophie didn't know if she'd ever get enough of his intensity.

"Between us. I'm not staying in Montana, probably… and, oh god…"

He bit her shoulder, crossing a hand to her other breast and pulling her nipple. Fire and ice collided on her skin and raced like gremlins over her nerves. She moaned, head thrown back as her brain crossed the threshold between restraint and not caring. His hands stopped and, in a flash, the only thing moving was Tucker's pounding heartbeat reverberating over her back like a drum.

• • •

He wanted to pull away from her, but he couldn't. All the care he'd taken to avoid this very problem. Never letting a woman get too close—never keeping one around long enough to get within an inkling of falling in love. But her question was open ended and he wasn't sure how to answer because nothing he said would be completely true. He didn't know what the hell he wanted. Tucker's cock jumped, screaming at him to lather himself all over Sophie and forget about problems. She sighed, a full-bodied, sad sound that made his heart race even faster. He didn't want her to be sad. He didn't want her to hurt, and he sure as hell didn't want her to fall for him, either.

"I can't do more than sex, Sophie." The words were meant to be a warning, but failed miserably. It was the easy way out, but better for her. He wasn't relationship material. Hell, he didn't even know if he *could* do a relationship even if he wanted to. Intimacy he knew and even though he'd broken his own damn rule about never keeping the same woman around, he had let it slide. Because, if nothing else, he needed this.

His hands began a slow draw over her ribs. He shouldn't touch her, but all the demons in hell couldn't stop him. She moaned, her body softening.

Her breathy voice stung him. "Good."

A surge of control pulsed through him. Good? What the hell did that mean? It should have given him relief that she wasn't in this for more, but…it didn't. Tucker shook off the disappointment. He was in control, and this would go his way because there wasn't another option. With a growl, he nudged Sophie against the tree until her arms buckled and her forearms rested against the bark. He took a long look at her naked ass, the soft round globes of her cheeks pale against the red triangle of her silky thong. He pulled the sides of the thong down, watching that little slip of fabric dance over her rear and collect against her thighs.

Her slight cry sounded like protest and encouragement rolled into one vibrating exclamation. Testing her, Tucker slid a hand between her thighs, gracing her soft curls with the side of his hand. She parted her legs immediately, and he smiled, feeling wicked and angry and wanting. Gripping the bunched dress in his left hand to hold her steady, he plunged two fingers inside her. Tucker swore. She was drenched, blasting heat and sweet wetness around his hand. Sophie leaned back, pressing her hips harder into the invasion.

"Sophie," he growled, losing his voice as he nipped the

skin over her spine. He found her slick nub, rubbed it until she ground down against the pressure. Holy shit, it wouldn't take much to make her come. Tucker's groin pulled, his lower abdomen clenching with heat. This is what he craved. This primal sex, the way she gave herself up to him. Sophie was woman enough to take what she wanted from him and strong enough to tell him when he was crossing the line. It was a sexual tug-of-war and he needed it like air.

Damn her.

He stroked her fast with just enough pressure to make her pant and groan and swivel her hips in time with his hand. He palmed her breasts, kissed her neck, while he struggled with a storm he refused to give name to.

"Why won't you…oh god," Sophie panted. "Why won't you let me touch you?"

Tucker pulled back from her clit, sliding his fingers inside her tight center with slow precision. The question floored him, but he wasn't going to give in. He was going to stay in control of this if it killed him.

"No touching."

When she breathed to speak again, he added another finger and thrust them hard. She sucked in a breath, uttered something nonsensical as he thrust again, harder until she cried out, her legs nearly giving way. Tucker braced her around the waist with an arm, pulling her back against his straining cock.

"No more talking." His fingers slid over her nub, resuming the strokes he knew unraveled her. The cadence of sound pouring out of her was the most beautiful music he'd ever heard. God, he'd never get tired of hearing her come.

"Tucker!" Sophie pressed her cheek against the tree. Her nub swelled beneath his fingers and Tucker closed his eyes, leaning low over her body so he could absorb every vibration, every soft sound. *Too fast*, he thought suddenly. *She's coming too fast.*

He pulled his hand away, taking a second to gather his breathing and get control. The ground seemed to spin, lifting him up into a funnel of pure adrenaline and lust. Sophie mewled in protest, her hips pushing back against him, seeking. She was panting for him, her body humming for him. He let his jeans open and slide down. One hand slid up her back, raking his nails back down as goose bumps claimed her skin. His other hand gripped her right hip as he brought them together. The movement of her chest caught and held as he slid inside. Sophie clenched tightly around him as she fought for her own control.

Tucker dipped his forehead to her back as his arm braced around her middle and he held them, connected in all ways, hearts beating in tandem. Her breath came out agonizingly slow; Tucker's chest clenched at the methodical slowness of it. When she muttered something that sounded like begging, he gave in, moved in long, hard thrusts. Sophie came undone, her arms braced against the tree as her bottom pressed against him again and again, seeking and finding, as her entire body seemed to release at once.

Tucker followed, coming hard to the furious pound of his heart and sudden weakness in every muscle. She'd reduced him to a boneless mass of feelings. *Jesus Christ.* He followed her to the floor, his arms banded around her, his body arched possessively over hers. A boom sounded above them. For a second, Tucker thought it was his heart.

"Fireworks," Sophie said quietly. She turned in his arms and pulled the flaps of her dress together. Tucker kissed her forehead and ran his fingers over the soft, milky white of her jaw. Still shaking, Tucker righted his clothes, helped Sophie do the same. And then they sat in the middle of the floor and looked up.

A crackle, a sparkle, and a burst of red, and blue and

yellow shattered above the skylight. Another boom, another vibration. Another brilliant display of color. A bright white explosion lit the sky followed but a series of quick multi-colored sparks. Sophie leaned her head on his shoulder and the war Tucker was fighting inside shattered like the night sky.

Chapter Twelve

Tucker paused at Sophie's front door. She stepped inside, tugging his hand, but he couldn't follow her. Pulled between frustration at his own weakness and the need to put distance between them, he allowed Sophie to lead him to the door, but that was far enough. If he went any farther, he might not leave.

Her face was lightly flushed, her eyes glowing with deep contentment. He could lose himself in her expression and roll around on the peaceful air surrounding her. There was something soft and comforting about Sophie that Tucker was starting to need. He thought about it in the middle of the night when he reached out and half-expected her to be lying there. He thought about it when he worked all day long, under the sun, the rain, the overcast sky. It didn't matter. Sophie was on his mind constantly and it was driving him mad. He didn't have time for this, but he sure as hell didn't know how to make it stop. Her time to leave Paint River couldn't come fast enough, as far as he was concerned. Out of sight, out of mind, he had no doubt.

"Do you want to stay a while?" She kicked off her sandals. The straps slid slowly over her delicate ankles and down to the tips of her blue-painted toenails.

Tucker licked his lips, forcing his gaze to settle on the generic wall art above the flat screen television. "I can't stay."

She tucked hair behind one ear, showing off the peachy flush on her cheek. Long eyelashes fluttered over her eyes, but not before he saw the disappointment there.

"Okay."

She tucked hair on the other side, revealing a scuff on her cheek that looked remarkably like stubble-burn. Tucker touched his jaw, knowing full well he'd shaved before he picked her up tonight. With a cascade of guilt, he recalled pushing her against the tree. She'd cried out; he'd thought it was from passion. Tilting his head to get a better view of the angry scratch, he realized he'd hurt her.

Hurt her. Ground her face into the tree trunk, blinded by his desperate need for her and oblivious to the fact he was rubbing her skin over the bark like a cheese grater. *You dickhead*, he scoffed internally, *thinking about yourself, not her*. A selfish, bastard move.

His fingertips snaked out to trail along the edges of the abrasion. Sophie jerked at his touch, her hand curling around his. "What is it?"

"You...have a scratch." His emotions often burst into full potency before he even knew what was happening. When he felt, he *felt*. Turning inward was his method of choice for dealing with emotions he didn't want to face or let loose. Being with her in the tree house brought out feelings he swore he'd never feel again. Instead of facing it, he drowned them out by allowing his lust for her to overtake everything. And he'd hurt her—his selfish need hurt her. He couldn't do this, couldn't risk that he would hurt her more in some way, and watch the light in her eyes turn dark.

"Is it bad?" She scowled. *Yes it's bad*, he wanted to shout. This was bad. His most potent fears were seeing the light of day: if he let someone get too close, he'd hurt them, push them away, and make them want to run, with his temper, his selfishness, his indifference. Allowing lust to overtake Sophie proved it. Her face proved it. He wasn't capable of caring for someone else this way, of having to worry about their best interests or what they might want or need. Looking out for himself and his family was enough. There wasn't room for Sophie, not when it meant he'd likely end up crushing her, the way his father crushed everyone around him.

"Sophie," Tucker faltered with the release of her name. The sound of her cell phone ringing saved him from forcing the rest out. She jumped and grabbed the phone off the arm of the sofa. Glancing at the number with a furrowed brow, she looked apologetically at him.

"I've got to take this," she waved with her fingers. "I'll see you later." Then Sophie turned her back and answered the call. Tucker frowned. Phone call or no phone call, he had to cut their ties. She'd dismissed him instead of offering for him to wait until her call was done, a good sign, he thought, that maybe she needed space from him. The thought wasn't a pleasant one. Turning and walking out, Tucker locked Sophie's door from the inside before closing it. First thing in the morning, he'd tell her they were done. He'd had what he wanted, and this had gone far enough.

Still, the abrasion on her face killed him. He'd been too rough with her; too selfish with his own desire. For years, he'd run interference on all the nasty shit that went down behind the scenes at Paint River. Through it all, he stood rock-solid and absorbed the emotions of his family like the ground took in a beating storm. He didn't offer advice or comfort really, because he didn't know how other than to just *be* there—to be present—and, for the most part, that seemed to be enough.

So shoot him that he went where he wanted, did what he wanted to do, and answered to no one. Damn fine, that kind of freedom. No woman to tie him down; tell him when to be home or ask where he was going. No kids to worry about. There was nothing to answer to except the occasional face-off with Cole, and the demands of the ranch. That he could handle. The ranch didn't get emotional or want to cuddle, for God's sake, or need a hug. The cows and horses did what he wanted them to, and if they didn't cooperate? He'd just kept on them until they cracked.

He liked his life this way, and it wasn't going to change. Because he'd loosened up a little with Sophie, and look what happened. She had a big old scratch on her beautiful face, and proved exactly why he needed to stay away.

• • •

Dazed didn't even begin to describe how Sophie felt as she ran into the hospital, nearly knocking Carla over as she rushed into her mother's room.

"What the hell, Sophie?" Carla shouted, grabbing her by the shoulders, a furious twist on her lips. Deep lines branched out from the corners of Carla's brown eyes. "How many times did I call you? How many times?"

"I-I'm sorry," Sophie stammered, desperate to get out of Carla's grip so she could get to their mother's bedside. "I didn't have my phone with me." Guilt grabbed her by the throat. Sophie tried to shake it off and force her composure into submission, but her heart was the submissive one. Guilt was a heavy master and she was bowing deeply under its weight.

She'd known better than to attempt to lighten up her life. Tucker was a sweet distraction, but she'd taken him too far. Instead of paying attention to what her mother might need, or what might happen, she'd been wrapped up in a six-foot-three cowboy with magic hands and a sizzling wit that made her feel like maybe, maybe, life could be enjoyable again. Like maybe there was hope.

And then her mother had been rushed to the hospital—had needed her—and Sophie hadn't been there. Again.

Carla's fingers dug into Sophie's shirt, abrading fabric against flesh. "She could have died and you wouldn't have been here." She stormed into the hospital room, leaving Sophie panting under a wet blanket of heavy conscious. When she'd seen Carla's phone number flash on her phone, Sophie knew something had happened. Tucker was all but forgotten as her sister's words slammed into her: *significant stroke...brain hemorrhage...blood clot...* For the second time in one day, she'd driven blinded by emotion to her mother's bedside.

Arms crossed over her heart, Sophie padded softly into Violet's room. The lights were low and soothing, while a cardiac monitor beeped softly next to the bed. Violet lay still and ghostly, her skin a shade lighter than it had been that morning. Deep gray crescents lay in the hollows beneath each eye, her cheeks deeply pitted beneath facial bones that shouldn't have been poking out that far. Sophie crouched down beside the bed and gingerly took her mother's hand, afraid to squeeze or apply any pressure lest she shatter the fragile bones.

Carla was slowly pacing the room. "The blood clot moved. The doctor said it's only a matter of time now." The floor wobbled beneath Sophie's feet. She grabbed the mattress to steady herself.

"The clot didn't cause the stroke, but it moved into a spot that will eventually cause another one. A bigger one." Carla's sad eyes caught Sophie's over the bed. Her lowered voice was barely audible. "A month, maybe a little more, maybe less. Dr. Peterson said we should be prepared for her to slip quietly, when the time comes."

Looking at her mother was too painful. Sophie's gaze slid to the cardiac monitor. Her brain sank into the soft green glow of the screen and the black blips creating a little graph with every beat of Violet's heart. Sophie was familiar with the monitor, had used one similar on the ambulance. Right now it was a distraction instead of soothing proof that, if nothing else, her mother's heart was strong.

A strong heart wouldn't save her when the clot lodged itself inside a vein and stopped blood flow. Nothing would save her then.

"They are moving her back to the nursing home tomorrow." Carla's voice jostled the tears building inside Sophie's chest. They rose like an inverted waterfall up her throat and fell from her eyes. Violet had a do-not-resuscitate order, a directive she'd made legal when she was healthy, that no life-saving measures should be taken to prolong her life. Since she'd be waiting out her last moments on earth, without intervention, there was no reason to stay in the hospital. Sophie let her tears fall, managed a short nod of understanding.

They sat in silence in the dim light. Monitors beeped, voices spoke in low tones outside in the hallway. Sophie watched the floor as tears dripped off her nose, grateful her sister couldn't see. Tears came more often for her than Carla, had as long as she could remember. It was just another reason for Carla to scoff, and though life had toughened Sophie greatly in her adult years, she didn't want her sister to see an old weakness.

Finally, Carla cleared her throat. "I've requested the garden room for Mom at the nursing home. It's the best room in the facility—complete with a private one-on-one nurse, and a full view of the Japanese gardens. I already made the down payment so she can be moved as soon as it's available."

Sophie quietly wiped her face with her hands. "I didn't know there was a garden room."

"She loves gardens; she'll love this room." Sophie couldn't argue, despite the fact that Violet would never waken to see the room, or the garden. If there was peace and comfort to be found there, Sophie knew that would be good enough.

"It's expensive, Sophie." Carla stood and looked out the window overlooking the city. "I'm going to need you to help me out a little more." Sophie paused with her mouth half open. A strangled sound made its way past her lips, her hands splaying wide. Money, at the moment, was cause for white-flag waving panic. She didn't have any and didn't have a way of getting more.

"Carla, I've given you everything I have." She looked up, caught her sister's hard gaze. Whispering, her voice thick with tears, Sophie shook her head, "I'm broke." Even as she said the words, Sophie knew she'd find a way. Violet deserved the best. If she could make her mother's last days peaceful and sublime, Sophie knew she'd donate her own organs to make it happen.

"Sophie, we agreed that we'd split all of this fifty-fifty."

Sophie gave a dismissive wave of her hand. "I'll figure it out." She scratched the back of her neck. Carla sighed deeply and turned back to the window. "Good old resourceful Sophie." Her condescending tone cut Sophie deep and, if she weren't so upset, she would have given in to anger. Instead, she resumed rubbing the back of Violet's hand with her thumb. Scooting back in her chair a bit, Sophie leaned over the mattress until her head tucked against her mother's arm, just as she used to do as a child.

"Are you finally going to stay in Missoula?" Carla's soft voice had a slight waver. Sophie didn't look up. She let her cheek sink into the soft mattress that smelled like antiseptic and baby powder. She hoped that Violet's nightgown might smell like her old perfume, but the scent of hospital and stringent laundry detergent permeated the fabric.

"Yes." She closed her eyes. She sank into her mother's faint warmth and the steady but slow rhythm of her breathing. Even if she had a job to go back to, Sophie knew there was no way in hell she could leave now. She'd left too many times before when she should have stayed. There wasn't time to make the wrong choice anymore.

Violet had taken care of her and Carla all these years as a single mom. No, now it was all about Violet. There wasn't room for anything else. With a deep sigh, Sophie felt the last of her tears dissolve as a plan started to form in her brain. A plan that included a lot of work and no time for Tucker. Best to break it off now so she could dive in headfirst and be the daughter her mother desperately needed.

A light touch on her shoulder made Sophie look up. Carla stood next to her with tears rolling down her cheeks.

"You'll stay with me a couple days, okay? Until we get her settled back at the rest home?"

Wordlessly, Sophie reached up and gripped Carla's hand. Carla's fingers went rigid, her flesh cool, but she didn't pull away. After a moment, her hand softened and Sophie squeezed it harder as they each gave in to their own quiet storms of emotion.

Chapter Thirteen

Tucker stepped into the office with a stack of receipts for Paint River's receptionist. He could count on one hand the number of times he'd been in the office. The very idea of paperwork and ringing phones inside the small space made him want to twist a nut before spending any time there. With everyone gone today, he had no choice.

Taking off his hat, he stood by the deserted desk. A couple different girls shared the full-time position, but he couldn't recall their names. He was unfamiliar with the inside staff, a sudden thought that gave him pause. In the time he'd been shouldering most of the operational responsibility, he probably should know more of the interior staff by name. A soft, desperate voice came from behind the divider wall that separated the front office from the back. The desk phone rang, flashing with a red light on the switchboard.

Tucker frowned, leaning slowly to the right to try and peek behind the divider wall for the sound of the voice. A girl with a mop of brown curls twirled out from behind the divider, her eyes growing huge when she saw him. She made a mad lurch for the switchboard phone and dropped her cell phone at the same time.

"Mr…Mr. Haywood!" she squeaked. The phone stopped ringing, a click sounding through the room as voicemail switched on. Tucker couldn't remember meeting her, though she knew him. Her eyes were damp and red-rimmed, a fact she tried to hide by dipping her head and grabbing a tissue. A little throb started behind his left eye at the sight of her tears. Shit, he didn't even know her and her emotions were affecting him. The urge to race out the door almost got the best of him, but he pressed his heels into the carpet and gritted his teeth.

"Everything okay?" The words were forced, but he got them out. Tucker put the stack of receipts on the desk and she took them with a trembling hand.

"I'm sorry about the-the phone." Her voice was thick and she refused to look up. It took him a moment to realize she thought he'd care that she hadn't answered the switchboard phone. He glanced at her nametag. Stacy Kane. "It happens, Stacy." He replied, the anxiety welling in his gut at her continued puffy eyes and red-streaked cheeks getting stronger. "Um, is there something I can, you know, help you with? You seem…upset."

She wiped her nose with a tissue. "It's just, my babysitter just called and my son has a high fever and keeps falling asleep and, Mrs. Haywood is out and I can't…can't find anyone to come in for me and my husband is over-the-road…" The fast pace of her words nearly made his head spin. He put his palms out in the only attempt he knew to calm her down.

"Hey, hey… Go ahead." He pulled a tissue from the box on the counter and held it to her. She looked up at him with a dubious expression.

"What's that, Mr. Haywood?"

He almost laughed at the formality. Mr. Haywood was his father, not him. "There's an evening girl that comes in later, right?"

"Yes, she'll be here at five. She couldn't come in now because she has a morning job…"

"Go ahead. I've got this." He couldn't believe the words as they flew out of his mouth. He'd be alone, in this cubicle with narrow walls and one window. He almost groaned. The tissue she was holding floated down from her hand. "Are— are you sure you know how to do this?" she blurted, her cheeks instantly flaming red.

"I just answer the phone, right?"

"Well, yes but if it's a reservation, you need to know how to book that. And if a guest needs assistance, you need to call Brent to take care of it. Guest calls come in on this switchboard here, and other calls here." She pointed to two separate panels. "For Brent, push number 25."

"Tell you what. I'll just take messages unless it's a guest needing something, and the night girl can take care of it later. In the meantime, go get your son." Relief flooded her features, giving him an odd sense of pride that he'd done something to make her feel better. There, that hadn't been so hard, he supposed. His head hadn't exploded and she hadn't run out of here in tears. She grabbed a bag from beneath the counter and slung it over her shoulder. Then, grabbing a thin stack of pink slips, she held them out. He took the slips with a pluck of his thumb and forefinger and held them at arm's length as if they were dripping poison.

"These are phone messages for guests. Their name and cabin number are on the back. Brent can deliver them for you." She moved to come around the counter, paused, and went back to the computer with a little hiccup. "Oh, Ms. Miller in eighteen just called. She'll be out for a few days and believes she forgot to lock the cabin, so send Brent to lock it up."

He set the papers on the counter. Something in the

way Stacy said *Ms. Miller* concerned him. "Sophie Miller?" Sophie had been gone when he'd went around to her cabin earlier, dousing the need he had to see if the scratch he'd left behind was any better.

Stacy nodded with a frown. "Yeah. Poor thing…I felt sorry for her," she abruptly stopped talking, the blush returning to her pale cheeks.

Tucker stood a little straighter. "Why's that?"

Stacy nibbled her lower lip as if weighing the pros and cons of gossiping with the boss. "Well, she just sounded like she'd been crying is all. And she…she reserved the cabin until the end of the month. She said she had to max a credit card to do it. But it went through, so she's all paid up."

Stacy put a knuckle to her lips as if she'd said too much, but as far as Tucker was concerned, she hadn't said enough. Why was it so important for Sophie to stay here that she'd max a credit card to do so? This thing between them wasn't enough of anything to prompt her into hanging around…he'd told her that he wasn't good for more than sex. And while he might be pretty confident in his skills in that department, even he wasn't conceited enough to think a woman would throw all her cash away for a little more time with him.

So, maybe that thought did give him a moment of pure, self-absorbed male pride. Tucker blinked it away, his palm coming down on top of the slips on the counter. He might not be able to give Sophie much, but he could save her some cash. In fact, that same pride insisted on it.

"Take the charge off."

Stacy paused. "I'm sorry, but Mrs. Haywood would have to approve that."

"I'm approving it." The cold edge in his voice; the don't-question-me-or-else firmness that got him his way, had no place here, but it came out without thought on his part. It was natural, how he expected people to jump when he said go, even when he didn't intend to come across that way. Stacy stiffened and he was immediately regretful.

"Never mind, you go. I'll discuss it with the night girl. I hope your son gets better soon."

Stacy gave him a grateful, if cautious, smile and hurried out. The phone started ringing the minute the door closed behind her. Tucker stared at it as if projecting the reluctance he felt inside could magically make it stop. He let voicemail get it while he pondered what the hell was up with Sophie. He wasn't happy with how they'd parted ways last night. The protective side of him, one that shocked him to the core, wanted to snoop for her cell phone number and call her. The stony part of himself he was most used to didn't want to get involved. He went with the stony part as he sat in the cushy office chair, propped his boots on the desk, and dug a toothpick from his pocket.

He had no business worrying about Sophie, but he did. It wasn't just physical. He liked the sound of her laugh and her smile and the way she looked off into space when she didn't think anyone was looking. She carried herself with a stubborn throw-back of shoulders and ramrod spine, her chin jutting up as if she expected a confrontation at any moment; posture, he supposed, that came from dealing with tense, crazy, and morbid situations in her medic job. Yet, around the toughness was the undeniable softness of pure woman. A woman who loved to be held. One who liked to get her nails done, and had pretty colors in her hair and wore mind-blowing perfume. Sophie Miller was an enigma, both tough and soft and an all-city girl. Nothing he expected, and everything he shouldn't want.

He got up and paced a little, fiddling with things on the desk, feeling the walls closing in on him. Damn office. He should be on his horse or working alongside Jax, anything but sitting in this cracker box with a fake plant on the counter and barely any sunlight streaming in.

"Tucker?"

He looked up as Maeve walked through the door, bringing a blanket of sunlight in with her. He sighed in relief until a bright glint caught his eye. He glanced at her left hand. A huge diamond ring winked back at him.

"What are you doing in here? Did you lose a bet or something?" His mother's lighthearted voice cut through the sudden clog in Tucker's brain.

"I'm…I…" He looked down at the ring on his mother's hand, then up to her face. She was glowing with an elated, gorgeous smile.

"Is Stacy here? She left a message on my cell saying she had to leave."

"I'm Stacy," he stammered. "I mean, I told her to go away. *Home.* I told her to go home."

Maeve's smile got bigger. "Wow, my Tucker is getting a soft spot for…"

"What the hell is that on your hand?"

Maeve's eyes softened as she stared at him. He waited, realized he was holding his breath when his chest started to burn. It didn't take a psychic to know. This had been coming a long time, they'd all known it, and with an honorable amount of time passed since her husband's death, there was no reason for Maeve not to move on with her life. A sudden sadness washed over Tucker, one he couldn't explain.

"Jim proposed." She tentatively slid her left hand across the counter. The huge, square-cut diamond caught every dim ray of sunlight and threw it all over the room. "He…he wanted to ask all of you boys for your blessing, but I…I didn't want to wait."

Tucker's scalp tingled as he contemplated Maeve's words. He was pretty sure she was speaking a foreign language. In all the years he'd known Jim, Tucker had clung to his laughter, kindness, and attention. It had been like a holiday when Jim would arrive from Chicago to the ranch for one of his extended, bi-yearly stays. He'd ride with Jim after chores were done, or simply sit next to him quietly at a bonfire, listening to stupid ghost stories, or Jim's sad attempts at playing Cole's fiddle.

Jim had been day to Cooper Haywood's night, and as hard as he tried, Tucker couldn't remember a day he hadn't wished Jim had taken Cooper's place.

Maeve splayed her hands with a sigh. Tucker realized he hadn't yet responded and didn't feel able to. "I know this seems sudden. But the truth is I've known Jim almost half my life. And I've loved him just as long." The plea for understanding, for acceptance, in her voice caused his inner sadness to grow deeper. Why he was feeling this way made no sense. Of course he was happy for his mother...after the hell she'd put up with over the years with his father, she definitely deserved happiness.

He tried to speak, but crossed his arms instead. In the span of a year and a half, Cole had remarried—having found his soul mate in Rylan—and Maeve had fallen in love again. They were moving on, his family, finding a new way. Taking second chances and coming out ahead.

Almost as if she was reading his thoughts, Maeve put an elbow on the counter and reached her other hand to smooth a chunk of hair from his brow. That simple gesture could reduce him from grown man to little boy, every time. It was her trademark soft touch, her way of trying to smooth his ruffled feathers. "Tucker, I deserve this chance at happiness."

Yes, she did. Tucker caught her hand before she could fiddle with his hair again, drew her knuckles to his lips for a soft kiss. She deserved the world, and as much as he wanted to congratulate her, he couldn't get past the bowling ball in his throat. Worse was that he didn't know exactly why the joy he wanted to feel wouldn't come to the surface. Instead of disappointing her with whatever word salad might come out of his mouth, Tucker touched her cheek, tipped his hat, and walked out.

Sunshine hit him hot and bright, flooding him with the relief of being out of that small space. But breathing didn't get any easier. His chest still clenched hard, his gut a pit of unease and unnamable feelings. Hell, breathing be damned. It hurt too much to suck air into the empty cavity where his heart would be if it didn't feel like it had shrunk a couple of sizes and landed like a rock at his feet.

Chapter Fourteen

Sophie stayed three days in Missoula, dividing her time between sitting with Violet at the rest home, and scouring the want ads for a job. She and Carla had gone over the costs of keeping up with their mother's medical bills. More than once, Sophie almost broke into a fit of anxious tears, especially when Carla stood firm on wanting to move their mother into the Garden Room as soon as it became available. Sophie couldn't deny her mother that; she wouldn't deny her anything. After their financial powwow, it became apparent that she needed money as fast as she could earn it. Luckily, a varied employment history in her college years made her well-versed in the service industry. Finding a medic job in Montana would require applying for a transfer of her Minnesota paramedic license, and would take too much time.

It was summertime and tourists were in full swing. It only took one day of hard looking to find an evening gig waitressing at a bar called Tit for Tap. When she'd seen the ad in a college newspaper Carla picked up, she'd laughed. No self-respecting woman would work at a place with Tit in the name, but Sophie was too broke to be completely self-respecting. Besides, she'd done plenty of time waitressing at sports bars in the city where a well-placed smile and tight uniform shirt resulted in easy tips.

Despite the lurid name, the Tit for Tap was clean, well-organized and, according to the manager who'd interviewed her, was crazy busy Thursday through Sunday. The front seating area was huge, the bar flanked on the right by a generous stage, a billiard room bringing up the rear. Sophie shrugged off the crunch of peanut shells under her sandals and the short belly shirt she'd be required to wear. The place could get rowdy and a little rough thanks to the generous mix of local cowboys, curious tourists, and brave frat boys who co-mingled on any given night. But bouncers in every corner watched over the staff, especially the waitresses. She'd take her chances. The place screamed easy money, and she'd endure a little ass-grabbing to make sure she could provide for her mom.

She returned to Paint River late in the afternoon the day after her interview, having spent as much time as she could at the nursing home. She'd overshot that time a little, leaving her two hours before her first shift at the bar started. Luckily, Tit for Tap was only twenty minutes from the ranch. She'd rented the cabin at the ranch for a bit longer mostly because, though Carla had asked her to stay with her, Sophie was more at ease away from her sister's place. With any luck, she'd be able to find a place to rent soon. But for now, the cabin was convenient.

But while the cabin might be in a convenient location, it also kept her in the middle of Tucker's very tempting path. Her mother's declining health had given Sophie a single-minded focus: make money to keep her mother comfortable until her final days. Tucker Haywood was the kind of man she could fall for, no question. And falling was a luxury she couldn't afford. Though they'd both tiptoed around the sex-only thing, she couldn't even risk that anymore. Because the more time she spent with him, the more he touched her, the more clear the path to falling for the cowboy.

She stepped into a scalding shower, letting the heat permeate her deepest emotions through her skin, wishing the water could wash the anxiety away. She scrubbed head to toe with Margarita body wash and slathered coconut shampoo in her hair, letting the girly smells lighten her mood. By the time she dried off and painted her nails a bright shade of blue, Sophie was feeling a little more human.

She'd just slipped into the tiny black uniform shirt and a pair of low rider jeans when a knock sounded on the door. Threading a worn brown belt through the loops on her jeans, Sophie padded bare foot to the door, swinging it wide. She jumped to see Tucker leaning against the outside doorjamb, black hat pulled low, toothpick sticking from one corner of his beautiful mouth. A deep longing pulsed in her belly at the sight of him, the neatly-tucked reservations unfolding in a burst of confetti inside her heart. The top four buttons of his denim shirt were undone, while dusty, worn tan chaps were slung low on his hips. Day-old stubble swept his jaw and she itched to feel it under her fingers.

He swept her from feet to eyes with a slow moving, smolder of a stare. And then his eyes went huge and he took two big steps inside, slamming the door behind him.

"Oh hell no!"

• • •

Three days, he'd agonized that she hadn't come back to the cabin. Denial was a sweet mistress, allowing him to discount his disappointment during the day while he was busy. Checking on her cabin now, Tucker had a hard time admitting that he'd nearly shouted for joy to see her car parked in the drive. That joy was short-lived when he saw the black T-shirt clinging to her gorgeous breasts.

There was only one way she would have gotten her hands on that shirt—working at the Tit for Tap. Patrons could buy other shirts with the bar logo, but not ones like these. Oh no. These little black shirts were reserved for waitresses to flaunt.

"Why are you wearing that shirt?" He was growling and he knew it. Good. Maybe she'd realize how pissed he was and take the shirt off.

She crossed her arms. "Hello to you, too. Won't you come in?"

He ignored her sarcasm, tipping his hat back a little because it suddenly felt too tight. He wanted to demand where she'd been though he knew it was none of his damn business. While he'd been struggling with the fact that he actually *cared* that she'd been gone, she'd been prancing around at the Tit.

Tucker glared at the cropped black top with *Tit for Tap* lettering in silver glitter, wishing he could incinerate it with his eyes. His temple began to throb, the bounding pain reducing his ability to think of anything beyond the fact that Sophie was wearing that damn shirt. With nothing but skin underneath it, her bare, tight belly begged him to rake his fingers over it. As soon as she stepped into the bar, his wouldn't be the only fingers itching to get all over her.

"You're working there?" He gestured to the shirt. Hell, she looked good. Tucker didn't want to be pissed. He wanted to grab her in his arms and show her just how much he'd missed her. He glanced at her cheek where the scratch had been, relived to find it had healed. That flare of relief almost covered the deep angst her outfit caused him. Almost.

Sophie nodded. She hooked her thumbs in her front jeans pockets and gave him a curious look. "Yeah. I start tonight. In fact, I need to get ready, so maybe I can catch you later."

Her voice was hard, but her eyes were conflicted. Tucker saw the shine in them when she'd seen him at the door, the little flip of happiness that had alighted there. She didn't wait for a response, but turned and went to the bathroom. No way was he leaving before he'd had his say. Tucker followed her and leaned against the doorframe.

She looked at him in surprise, the warning in her voice was clear. "*Tucker.*"

He grinned, but she only scowled harder. Fine, she wanted to be stubborn, so be it. He'd beat her at that game every time. "You don't know what you're getting yourself into working at the Tit." He crossed his arms. He needed to stop this insane jealousy. Arguing with her about her choice of employment screamed intentions and relationships, things he couldn't touch. Yet, his heart wouldn't let it go. Sophie regarded him, cool and unruffled, before opening a drawer and pulling out a little fabric bag. She unzipped it and laid cosmetics out on the counter before dabbing white cream from a tiny glass jar beneath her eyes.

"The *Tap* isn't that bad. It'll be fine." She gave him a sideways glance in the mirror. He frowned. She wasn't taking this seriously and he sure as heck was. Sophie poured a few drops of liquid from a small bottle with the words "Brazilian Silk" on the label, rubbed it between her hands, and then swiped them though her hair. He frowned. Nothing good could come from anything with the word, "Brazilian" in it. Whatever it was made her shine.

"It's not the place for a girl like you." That got her attention. Her stare burned him from the edge of the mirror before she looked away and smoothed a huge brush over her cheeks, leaving a light pink smudge behind. It was one thing that her belly showed in the space where her low-rise jeans started and the T-shirt ended just below her ribs. She had to put makeup on *and* fluff her goddamn hair, too.

"I need the money. " She said tightly. "You know what girls back home do when they need money?"

"Strip?"

She whipped him a look. "They work in a bar like the *Tap*. Cheap drinks, big tips."

Tucker talked right over her. "Strippers."

The cheek brush slammed down on the counter. She was angry, but the hint of desperation in her eyes hit him harder. He thought of her maxed-out credit card, realizing just how little he knew about what kind of difficulties she might be having.

"They *don't have* strippers at the Tap!"

"Might as well, for all the boob and ass grabbing that goes on. You'll see. The Tit for Tap is notorious for fondling fun. Ask any local, they'll tell you which girl to feel up first." If he'd thought that little tidbit would give her pause, he was wrong. She went on as if she hadn't heard him.

"The *Tap*."

"The. Tit."

"Ugh." Sophie rolled her eyes at him in the mirror as she stuffed the makeup brushes into the bag and crammed everything into a drawer. Her hair was glossy and smooth and she smelled like coconut with a hint of lime, like an intoxicating cocktail. The guys at the Tit were going to be all over her. Tucker's gut clenched with a new flood of anger. Sophie might not be his, but the thought of some redneck trying to cop a feel on her while she played nice to get big tips about drove him out of his mind. No way.

"Take off that shirt, Sophie."

Astonished wasn't quite the right word to describe the look on her face, right before it turned to pure indignation, and she laughed at him. Laughed. In his face. "Seriously, Tucker? Because I don't think so."

"Didn't they tell you how it works? Tit *for* Tap. A dude

wants a beer; he's got to grab a handful first."

Sophie crossed her arms over her middle. "*Pfff*, that's not true."

Tucker's face went hot. Oh it was true. He knew it well himself. The thought of Sophie being the object for another man's beer mongering nearly set him off in a rage. "It's very true. In fact, I can tell you right now which waitress's tits are real and which aren't. Want a list?"

Sophie gasped with a twist on her glossy lips. "You're an ass."

He mocked looking around for something to write with. "Don't worry, Fifi. I'll add you to the top of the list for 'very hot and very real.'" He wanted to stop her from doing this; wanted to shake some sense into her before she got in over her head. She was desperate enough for cash to work at the Tit, but why? He wanted to press for information, the sudden urge to just throw money at her stabbing through his brain. Tucker's shoulders snapped back at the thought. He'd never wanted a woman to have reason to use him for the ranch, his name, his money, and his affection. That he'd even thought about it now put a bad, bad taste in his mouth. This was going too far, but he cared. Damn it, he cared and that almost scared him more than Sophie leaving for the Tit for Tap. And what had caring got him so far?

A pissed-off Sophie who laughed at him and clearly had no intention of listening to reason.

Sophie turned off the vanity light and walked to the door. Tucker's eyebrows rose when she paused, waited for him to move so she could get past. When he didn't, she ducked her head and squeezed by.

"It shouldn't matter if I work at the Tap, Tucker," she threw at him as she popped out into the hallway. "It shouldn't matter to you what I do." No, it shouldn't. It really, really shouldn't if he knew what was smart for them both.

He chewed the toothpick with a sense of unfamiliar helplessness. Emotions flickered across her face, ending with a defiant set of lips and narrowed eyes that were sad, yet cool with indifference. Huh, he'd never seen that expression on her before. Sophie cleared the short space between them, one hand trailing softly over the buttons on his shirt. It seemed completely involuntary, this touch and she tried to pull back. But he gripped her elbow and pulled her closer.

"Tucker, listen." She tried to shrug off his touch, but he wouldn't relent. This isn't how he imagined their reunion would go at all. "I can't do this with you anymore."

He tugged her arm and pulled her against his chest. A soft sound escaped her as their bodies met and his right hand slid to the curve of her naked back. Her feminine scent swirled around him, tempting Tucker to bury his nose in her glossy hair and lose himself in her softness. His other hand pressed between her shoulder blades to draw her tight against his body. It was an unintentional embrace, but it fit and it felt amazing and he didn't want to let her go. Sophie exhaled and relaxed against him, her hands gripping his ribs and holding him just as tight.

"Are you sure about that?" he whispered against her hair. The words gave him pause, considering he had no intention of taking things further with her. His palms followed the contours of her spine to her bare midriff to her hips, and back up to her neck, each hand following the other in slow succession. Tucker moved his fingers just enough to drag a little pressure over her body, making her shudder and lean in closer. He groaned and dug his fingers into her hips. Her face tilted up and he grabbed the opportunity to capture her soft, glossy lips with his. Sophie deepened the kiss, pulling him closer with giant fistfuls of his shirt against his back. Triumph burst through him. She wanted him just as much as he wanted her. Now if he could just find a way of stripping that shirt off her and burning it without breaking the kiss…

Sophie drew back with a jerk. "Tucker, stop!" She wiggled until he loosened his arms and she could break free. Smoothing her hair with a shaky hand, Sophie took three steps back and glared at him with passion-filled eyes. "We can't do this…*that*…anymore." He made a move forward and she backed up again. "I mean it, Tucker."

"I'm up for the challenge." He paused at his own words. Jesus, she was giving him a no-apologies out and he wasn't taking it. Instead, all he could think about was keeping her close. His stomach bottomed out with the three-sixty going on in his head. It was the shirt…he was jealous over the thought of her wearing it in front of other men. There, man enough to admit it, but…

"This isn't a challenge."

"Sure it is. You want me. I want you. What's the problem?" What was the problem, his problem to be exact? He'd lost his mind…he should be ending things with her. Right now.

Sophie glanced at the ceiling with a short laugh. "This one-night-stand has gone far beyond the one-night rule. The problem is continuing to play with fire until one of us falls and the other one doesn't!" She spun away and leaned against the couch.

"Falls?" He pressed gently, already afraid of her response. A warm sensation melted through his chest at the idea that maybe Sophie already was falling. She peeked at him before pressing fingers to her brow.

"Yes, *falls*. Isn't that how a situation like this always ends?"

Tucker hooked his thumbs in the waist of his chaps, wanting to scoff at her words, but not quite being able to. She was being silly. And he was being stupid. He should have run out of here minutes ago, said thanks and good-bye, and never looked back. "There's no falling here, Fifi," he assured her. "Just pure, mutual, pleasurable-as-sin fun."

Tucker took a step to her, his palms itching to smooth over her naked belly. "Come on, it's fun for you too, baby. Look at you right now. Your skin is flushed all pink, the way it gets when I'm touching you. Your lips are wet from my kiss, parted just a little like they're begging for more." Sophie's mouth dropped open right before she snapped it shut.

Tucker took two more steps. "You get goose bumps when I touch you. Those beautiful tits? Swollen for my hands. You can't hide what you want from me, Soph." He stopped just close enough that her body heat wrapped around him. His cock jumped to full attention at the heady force of his words and the way desire displayed across her face in reaction. One more touch, and he could have her naked and moaning under him on the couch. Tucker fisted his hands, breathing deep to get himself under control.

Sophie swallowed hard. "I can't."

"You want to." He wanted to. Too much.

"It doesn't matter, Tucker." The steady heaving of her chest betrayed the inner workings of her struggle. Tucker gave her tiny Tit for Tap shirt one last cursory glance before grabbing his hat from the back of the couch and putting it on. He needed space to give himself a mental ass-kicking. Or before he hauled her over his shoulder and whisked her away somewhere—anywhere—to keep her from going to the bar.

"We'll see, Fifi." Tucker left and forced himself to go to the bunkhouse. He initiated a game of cards with Jax and cracked a new bottle of whiskey, the least he could do to stop himself from going to the Tit for Tap to watch the new waitress in action. If he did, there was no telling what kind of trouble he'd get into, and he was in trouble enough with that city girl already.

Chapter Fifteen

One good thing about many years of waitressing at bawdy, but lucrative bars is that Sophie didn't need any handholding to learn the ropes at the Tit for Tap. It was like every other bar she'd worked at: filled with a rowdy crowd that was half-drunk before they'd walked in, loud, and full of non-stop cat calling, ass-grabbing, stupid pick-up line fun. And not on her part.

She'd made three hundred dollars in tips her first night, and a touch more her second, so Sophie had high hopes for tonight, being Saturday. A line had formed outside the bar nearly an hour before it opened, with the craze starting on the street as impatient patrons threw beer cans at the Tit for Tap's front door and hollered to be let in. Bouncers had finally gone out for a little crowd control, but it hadn't settled Sophie's nerves much. She knew how to handle herself, sure, but being female in the middle of a crowd of men that boisterous and loud was a tad disconcerting, no matter how many other dives she'd worked in. Tucker had been right, though she'd never tell him. She wasn't cut out for a bar quite like this, but the past two nights had gone well and she'd already made enough to put a small dent in the fee for her mother's private room.

That was a good trade off, she figured. That, and holding her own so she could prove Tucker wrong. He'd infuriated her, demanding that she not work here, trying to strong-arm what *he* wanted into her life. He'd looked truly angry and concerned, which had taken her completely by surprise because they were, what, friends? Lovers? However it was defined, what they were didn't justify or explain why he'd feel protective over her, and yet, it had touched her anyway.

He cared.

It was scary and thrilling, and completely the fuel she'd needed to avoid Tucker at all costs the past two days. So she'd hung around Missoula until it was time to go to work, and then fell into bed at three in the morning afterwards.

Despite being around people all day and all night, she was lonely; she missed Tucker, and that just made her irritable. He wasn't supposed to care; that was getting too deep into something she couldn't reciprocate. Even if she wanted to, because she could...she *did*. And missing him implied that she wanted more, too, which clearly, wasn't possible. She was working at a bar with peanut shells on the floor and wearing a shirt that barely covered her boobs. If her life hadn't taken a misguided twist already, she hated to see what was in store next. But she would, and that was a path she'd take alone.

Sophie edged to the bar to grab her drink orders, ears perking up at the excited chatter between the lead waitress, Pasha, and another waitress, Bren. When Pasha grabbed her sleeve and tugged her sideways, Sophie was thrown into the conversation. Pasha had sparkly blond hair and warm brown eyes. She was thin enough to wrap her apron strings around twice, with a pretty flare of hips and breasts to fill her out just enough to make Sophie slightly jealous. Pasha's prettiness was the kind that could make her personality either incredibly bitchy or super sweet. She was both.

"Whatever happens, do not sit on the lap of the guy at table twenty." Pasha sighed longingly, but rolled her eyes, giving Sophie the impression that Table Twenty had some explaining to do.

She continued placing glasses on her tray with an indifferent shrug. Her motto was to get through bar hours and collect tips as quickly as possible. Not get involved in the drama around here. "Not my table, so I'm good."

"Not mine either," Pasha sighed disappointedly. "But I'm still hopeful."

Bren turned to Sophie. "Doesn't matter if it's your table or not. If he likes you, he'll pull you over and make you sit on his lap." She set a glass down with a resounding clank. "And then you'll sleep with him and never hear from him again. Not that I know from experience…unfortunately. But I've heard."

"Join the club, sister." Pasha slid an order pad in her apron pocket. "I've been trying to get a spot on his lap for over a year. No dice." Sophie made a quick glance through the bar. Why in the world would they be so worked up over a guy that sounded like a pump-and-dump? "He's sexy as hell and loaded on top of it," Pasha said, as if reading her mind. Then she made an "Mmmm-hmmm," sound like she was licking something delicious off her fingers, and nudged Sophie. "Don't say we didn't warn ya."

Sophie picked up her tray and waved Pasha on. "Good thing I'm not in the market for any lap-sitting." An image of long, muscled legs clad in denim and leather came to mind. Pasha just scoffed and held her tray high as she prepared to move through the access door.

"Yeah, well, Tucker Haywood will make you change your mind. Trust me."

The tray wobbled in Sophie's grip, drinks spilling over

and sloshing into each other. Tucker was at table twenty? Pasha grabbed her hands. "Whoa, Soph! You okay?" Okay was purely subjective. She could be okay that Tucker was a player because he wasn't hers and could do what he wanted. Or she could be okay by plastering on a happy face and pretend this news didn't bother her. Neither was working.

Everything seemed a bit numb, so Sophie set down the tray down before the whole damn thing fell over. *I can tell you which ones are real and which aren't. Want me to make you a list?*

"Oh *no*." Pasha gripped Sophie's shoulder with a squeeze. "You've already met him, haven't you?"

"What?" Sophie shook her head, denial trying to wiggle through.

"Tucker. You've already…ah, met him." Pasha watched her expectantly, but Sophie couldn't bring herself to respond. "He didn't make promises to you did he? I mean, that's not his normal. It's one-night. Any girl that's gotten tangled up with him usually knows that upfront, from what I hear anyway."

Sophie laughed a stunned, short sound. "Any girl?" No, he'd never made her promises, but their one-nighter had gone way beyond that and he'd never once put a stop to it. Neither had she.

Pasha clicked her tongue sympathetically. "He's kind of got a reputation. Sorry, Soph." With that, Pasha grabbed her orders and slipped away, leaving Sophie to wipe up her spills and pull herself together enough to sheepishly ask the bartender for do-overs. Swallowing hard, Sophie rooted herself to the floor and let a series of quick trembles wash over her.

Let it come and let it slide off your back. What Tucker did in his past, or his present for that matter, was no concern of hers. Yet the discomfort inside her heart had a pulse of its own and brought a wicked validity to what she was trying so hard to deny: she *was* falling for him. To her credit, she hadn't really had time to think things through. Stress could be driving this crazy attraction to him, or maybe the whole "forbidden fruit" thing was coming into play. Everyone wanted something they weren't supposed to have, right? Since the moment she'd spied him at the carnival and used him as a lifeline, Tucker had represented that one, luscious thing she couldn't have in the long term. Her life just wasn't at that point where a man should be hanging around, and she shouldn't encourage it.

Here she'd actually entertained the idea that he cared about her when, in reality, she'd just helped Tucker live up to his reputation. Sophie darted to the opposite end of the room from table twenty, not knowing, and trying hard not to care if Tucker was watching her from the shadows. Luckily, the bulk of her customers where a good distance away from where he was supposedly sitting, giving her berth to get her feelings, and her focus, under control.

She'd barely made sense of the anger and disappointment knocking around in her head when Pasha grabbed her arm and pulled her close to be heard over the DJ.

"You made it three days, so you have the chance to earn a little bonus. It's an initiation thing," Pasha said with a wicked smile. "Plus, the manager will give you a two-hundred-dollar bonus to do it." She hitched a thumb at the tiny platform next to the DJ stage. "Just got to get up there and dance. One song."

Sophie brushed Pasha's off. "Shut up."

"Not kidding." Pasha looked to Dave the manager, who waved a bill in the air with a wink.

"I dance on the stage and I get two hundred bucks?" She needed the money, and she knew how to dance. This was a no-brainer. She'd danced in front of more crowds than she could recall in all her years of dance, but never in a bar, and

never while wearing a belly shirt that barely covered her girls. Tucker's stripper comment came back to haunt her, and she gritted her teeth. She wouldn't be taking any clothes off, but she could shimmy for a couple hundred. Cash was her focus, after all. No harm in that.

"Yep. The crowd digs it. Dave knows he'll make the money back easy, plus some in drinks once you start shaking your ass up there."

Sophie wanted to blurt out that this was going to be the easiest money she ever made. Sixteen years of professional dance made stage fright a non-variable. "I get to choose the song?"

Pasha shrugged. "Yeah."

Sophie didn't want to sound too eager, but her quick, "You're on!" made Pasha clap excitedly. She was feeling a little of that excitement, too, over getting up there and dancing for the sake of her lost art. Yet Sophie couldn't help but think how much she'd rather be slow dancing with Tucker in the barn again, then shaking her ass in front of all these men. Her head was still crowded with images of him pulling some random woman on his lap, pumping a defiant kind of jealousy through her.

"Awesome. Tell the DJ your song and get on up there."

A chill burned her arms. It had been a while since she'd danced. To say she missed it was an understatement. After confirming the DJ had her song, she perused the crowd until she found a man wearing a baseball hat. He was more than agreeable to let her borrow it.

Sophie took her hair down, donned the cap and kicked off her flats before stepping up onto the platform. The crowd burst into the loudest raucous she'd heard in the three days she'd been working here. She put a finger to her lips to signal silence. To her surprise, the crowd hushed. Sophie felt a rush of adrenaline at the promise of a performance and hoped like hell she remembered all the moves to this routine. It was the last one she'd taught her teenaged hip-hop class at the dance company before she'd quit. With a tip of her other hand, Sophie signaled the DJ and Kesha's "Tik Tok" blasted through the room. Her face flushed at the murmur that went through the bar. Yeah, hip-hop in a country bar probably wasn't the best idea, but it was her favorite and she was good at it.

When she did a twisty, sassy walk across the platform, tipping the baseball hat to one side, the murmur turned into a cheer and her fears were forgotten, replaced by an adrenaline rush that erased everything in the room. For the first time in too long, it was just her and the music.

• • •

Tucker stood so he could see over the crowd. Up until every man in the room gathered around the stage, he hadn't been paying much attention. He'd been watching Sophie from the shadows, nursing a beer, but got sidetracked when a fellow rancher sat down for a chat. He wasn't being a stalker, really. He'd just wanted to check in, make sure she was doing okay at this shithole bar. The moment Tucker had set foot in the Tit for Tap, he was reminded that it had been months since he'd been inside, and for good reason. The dim atmosphere and loud, obnoxious crowd didn't hold any appeal to him anymore. Once, this was his spot of choice for getting away from the ranch, maybe finding a little female company. But it had lost its appeal, and he'd been quickly reminded why.

When he saw Sophie on the platform, rampant shock and disbelief quaked through him. What the hell? He knew rookie waitresses had to do a stint on the stage, but he'd never thought she'd do it. Oh, hell no. He'd come because he had to see her, and not to watch her sell herself out in

Dave's sleazy money-making trick. Tuck elbowed his way closer to get a better vantage point. She'd let her hair down, kicked off her shoes and was wearing a baseball cap. Then music with a vicious beat pummeled through the room and she just started dancing, in a fluid, yet controlled way that looked like something he'd see on television. It happened fast, each movement in perfect time with the music, the result impressive and oddly beautiful. Most of the girls he'd seen on this stage danced like barely-practiced strippers. Sophie was anything but, far surpassing what the Tit had seen before.

When she spread her arms wide, shook her chest and tipped the hat, the guys around the stage started fighting themselves to rush her. Sophie hopped backward, spreading her legs with knees bent and arching her body forward in a wide arc before jumping back and slicing the air with a fist. Tucker forgot about the men panting over her for a minute when he realized how fierce his normally soft Sophie looked. She exuded another identity, one that fit that inner spark he'd seen peeking from beneath her outward layers.

The naked strip of belly between her top and jeans glimmered in the light like her skin had been rubbed with oil. The light ends of her hair swayed around her shoulders and whipped around her face as she danced, her arms graceful yet purposeful, every sway and arc of her hips doing strange things to his gut. He knew her spark all right, and it took everything in him not to drag her off the stage right then and turn it into an explosion.

By the grunts and cheers of the men around him, he wasn't the only one thinking about doing naughty things to Sophie. Tucker bristled as jealously breeched the cage around his resolve to be indifferent. It was all he could do these past couple nights to stay at the ranch. But the image of other men groping and grabbing her while demanding drinks kept replaying in his mind. Yeah, coming here tonight wasn't a choice. It was a matter of keeping his sanity. If he didn't, he'd paced Paint River until Jaxon knocked him out cold, just to put him out of his misery.

Suddenly, the tempo changed, morphing into a seductive beat. One quick look to the bar displayed Dave, rolling a finger in the air at the DJ to keep him playing, likely with the hopes Sophie would keep dancing. The wall of men hadn't thinned any, making it difficult for Tucker to get closer. Sophie had stopped and taken off the hat, one hand smoothing back her hair as the other tried to wave off a wad of bills being offered her way from the crowd. Like a virus, the bill waving caught on and soon the front row was waving money like flags. She tried to discourage them, but the bastards weren't getting the message. When her brow fell and a flicker of fear crossed her face, Tucker elbowed his way through.

Before he could get there, a man jumped up on the stage. Sophie turned with a reluctant smile and set the baseball cap on his head. Apparently, that simple gesture was all the encouragement the Mets fan needed to take Sophie's hips in his hands and make a lewd gesture at her with his tongue. Dave better get his mop bucket ready, because shit was about to fly. Seeing red was appropriate, because all Tucker was thinking about was watching blood gushing from the Mets guy's face after he popped him a good one.

Someone moved a chair in his path, but he whipped it furiously to the side, ignoring the curse and clamor that followed. He tunneled in on the man looking at her backside like it was a delicious treat. A foot from the stage, someone grabbed Tucker by the arm. He spun, hands clenched and jerked to a halt when he saw Pasha with a stubborn frown on her face.

"No way. You're not going up there."

"Like hell!"

"Don't make me threw you out of here." She nodded to

the bouncer near the stage. Tucker knew one indication from her and he'd be out on his ass. So what. Just let them try to bounce him before he'd gotten Sophie down. Pushing past Pasha, he stormed to the platform. If Sophie was relieved to see him, she didn't show it. She said something to the Mets guy, but he didn't back off. The crowd squeezed around Tucker, hooting and cat-calling and cheering the Mets guy on. He was about to step up on the platform when someone bumped into him, driving him back. He ignored it, forged ahead until he was back at the platform. Sophie had moved a little closer to the edge as she twisted out of hat guy's grip. Tucker snagged her hand.

He gave her a little pull. "Get down from there Fifi."

"Tucker!" She tried to pull back, her expression clearly furious. Her anger fueled his to the limit. Was she actually mad that he was trying to break up the private show the Mets guy was after?

Tucker tightened his grip. "I said get down."

The man behind Sophie stepped forward with his shoulders squared and jaw set. Tucker bristled, every inch of his body hollering that he get up there and start swinging. He held himself back by a very thin and frayed thread of self-control, because he never swung first, but he also never backed down once fists started flying.

"Back the hell off or it won't end well for you."

Sophie put her free hand on the man's chest and shoved hard. He stumbled back, clearly not expecting her to push him away. The roar from the crowd turned into laughter.

"Why the hell do I need to get down?" She braced her feet and tried to pull back. Whatever game she was playing right now was not cool. Not cool at all. The apprehension on her face had been plain to see when the attention she was receiving got to be too much. And here she was, bucking him.

His patience was about done. "Because I told you to,

that's why!"

"You do *not* tell me what to do, farm boy." Farm boy. Tucker tipped his head back and braced his feet, prepared to pull her clear off the stage for that little blow. He saw the bouncer from the corner of his eye, but it didn't quell his anger any less. He wanted her out of here, away from these men.

When he just stood there, Sophie started to fidget. "Stop it. You're making a scene!"

Tucker yanked. Sophie fell forward off the stage and right into his arms. Tucker held her tight. "You're worth it." She stood completely still in his embrace, her forearms braced against his chest and her eyes bound to his. The crowd around them faded from loud voices and the rustle of crunching bills, to nothing but the sound of her fast, hard breathing and the pummel of his own pulse against his veins.

Tension coiled in her so tight, it might be impressive to see her anger really unleash. But she was mad at him, which wasn't what he'd intended, but he wasn't sorry. Sometimes anger was a byproduct and he wouldn't apologize for wanting her out of this bar. Maybe that made him selfish—okay, it did—but he didn't give a flying fuck.

"My god, Tucker. You're going to get me fired!"

He almost laughed. Did she really think that mattered one bit? "Obviously, I don't care."

Sophie pulled away and bar sounds seeped back in, reminding Tucker that they had an audience. A big one. He was grateful when she spun and stomped off. He followed her, each step cooling his temper, but not his need to make her understand…

Understand what, exactly?

He caught Sophie's arm gently when she slipped into an empty hallway that lead to the kitchen. She spun, making it easy to press her back against the wall. Talking wasn't getting him anywhere, and he didn't know what to say anyway, so he'd just have to show her.

Her fingers wrapped around his wrists in a fluid choreography as he took her face between his hands and wedged a knee between her legs. A fluttery gasp that sounded a lot like, "yes," came from her lips right before he ground his mouth to hers. It wasn't seductive, or soft, the way he kissed her. It was possessive and raw, an erotic communication that spilled out of him, claiming him in the process. Because this was caring. This was connection. This was wanting more.

More Sophie. Sophie in his bed, his home, by his side.

God, this was what his brother had…what his mother was holding by the hand, and Tucker wanted it, too.

The interior of her lower lip was velvety soft when he ran the tip of his tongue there. A small groan escaped her, her body arching away from the wall until their chests touched. His hands slid down her neck, taking on the curve of her shoulders to the narrow line of her ribs and curve of her waist. He'd had her, sure, but he didn't know her body, not the way he wanted to. Each line and dip and arch; he wanted them imprinted in his mind like a map, the kind that lovers made of each other when sex turned into a lifetime.

He pulled back, panting, heart full and racing to the point his chest actually hurt. He'd had that once and he'd walked away…still. Sophie's arms went to her sides, her palms going flat against the wall as if to keep from touching him. She didn't look mad anymore, but seemed just as conflicted as he felt.

"You need to go home, Tucker." There was a distinct tremble to her voice and for the first time, he was a little sorry for being so caveman with her earlier. There was probably another way he could have handled that, but whatever.

"I hate it that you're working here." What was the point in hiding from her anymore? He still wasn't sure what was going on inside him, but it wanted out.

Her shoulders moved in a boneless shrug. "Why? Why the hell does it matter?" His fingers threaded through the hair at her temples, fast and strong, pulling her to him with a renewed flare of emotion. *Everything she does matters to me.*

"I want you Sophie." The words tumbled out. "I don't understand it, but that's all I know…that I want you to *be* with me." A beat passed between them as he searched her eyes. Sophie ran a palm over her lips and turned her head to the tune of his heart dropping to his feet. The deep breath she took sounded ripe with brewing tears.

"We can't do this right now. Go home, Tucker."

"Sophie—

"Please." Her plea didn't move him into action, but the broken way she said it did. He'd spent his entire life afraid of not being able to give people what they needed emotionally, or not recognizing what they needed in return. He'd handled this whole thing badly and he was trying, really, dammit, trying to be sorrier about that.

If she needed him to walk away, he would. Every muscle in his back, legs, and neck were screaming to stay right where he was, but he backed up so Sophie could push away from the wall. And then he swept his thumb over her kiss-swollen lower lip, ignored the ache in his groin and his chest, and left.

Chapter Sixteen

Sophie climbed to a perch on the metal fence as Tucker reined the horse he rode sharply to the left. Exhausted from working the night before and attempts to sleep that equaled one big fail after that, her brain began to perk up at the sight before her. He rode the black and white horse bareback, his long, leather-clad legs showing off strong thighs. Sweat coated the back of Tucker's gray T-shirt, allowing the material to cling to every dip and rise of muscle. He was hatless today, the sun highlighting streaks of blond and copper in his mahogany hair.

Her heart was equally filled with elation and the weight of regret. Not only did he look incredible on that horse, Tucker was a really good man. The kind that women lined up to find and fought each other for a chance to be with. And he'd said he wanted her. Of all the women in Montana, he'd chosen her.

And she couldn't choose him back. The metal railing was warm from the sun as she gripped it hard. Two things summed up her life right now: the impending death of her mother and the uncertainty of her future. Both brought enough anxiety to kill a bull. Though being here at Paint River gave her a wonderful sense of peace, Sophie was aware it wouldn't last. Her time here would end, her mother would pass, and, eventually, Sophie needed to find a way to start her life over. Working at the Tit for Tap was temporary. And after that? She really, truly had no idea.

Tucker's brow was dipped in concentration as the horse went through a series of paces. The animal flicked his ears back and forth. She knew squat about horses, but those crazy ears just made the horse look cranky. First the horse walked, then jogged a little, and then started running in a circle around the corral. If Tucker had seen her on the fence, he didn't make any acknowledgement. With a soft command, he pulled back slightly on the reins and the horse tossed his head like a stubborn toddler. Tucker's thighs clenched, his lower legs moving back just a bit, hands going forward. The animal's body bunched, his flanks quivered like he was chasing off flies, tail swapping sharply against his belly.

Tucker made a sound, maybe a vocal command, Sophie didn't know. His legs repeated the same movement and he gave a click of his tongue.

And then the horse lost it.

The animal reared with another flick of his tail, head slashing side to side. Sophie cried out, but Tucker held on like the pro he was. Hooves hit the ground hard. One leg kicked out as his ears laid flat. Tucker flipped off sideways and managed to land on his feet, sending a puff of dirt up onto Sophie's boots. Her stomach clenched, momentarily taking her mind off the reason she'd come looking for him.

He spun when he realized Sophie was on the fence behind him.

"Oh my gosh, Tucker, that horse is—"

He walloped his hat against his knee before throwing it

on his head. "A son of a mother-effing-piece of fuc—" His face was set hard as he stifled the string of curses and drew a hand across his nose and mouth. "Stubborn!" he growled. "Pana bar Noir is stubborn."

"I was going to say beautiful."

Tucker's lips pinched into a hard, white line. Sophie chuckled, tried to hide it with her hand. She'd been a little worried he was hurt, but it was apparent his pride was the only thing bruised. When he narrowed his eyes at her, she giggled again. She expected him to be upset with her over the way they'd left things last night and the light of good humor behind his irritation at the horse was good to see.

Tucker turned away to grab Pana's reins. "You got something to say to me, woman?" He cocked his head with a glimmer of a grin.

"Why is this poor horse so far away from the yard?" The pen was tucked down below a gentle incline that lead to a thick row of trees. Branches overhung a small strip of the pen providing shade and the tinkle of aspen leaves in the breeze. She'd gone down to the barns and asked around for Tucker. No one seemed to know where he'd gone until a ranch hand had pointed her down here. With the gentle breeze and quiet, she couldn't blame him for choosing this place today.

"Because Pana's in bad-horse solitary, that's why. The farther away from distraction he is, the better he learns something new." He reached Pana and led him over. Despite the violent dance just moments ago, Pana stood calmly, head low, ears resting to the side. "He's still recovering from his accident. Being one-on-one with me soothes him. Makes him easier to handle."

Sophie jumped down from the fence and reached a tentative hand to stroke Pana's nose. "Accident?" She was amazed at how smooth and silky the horse's fur was, how velvety his lips felt when they blubbered over her palm, looking for a treat. She laughed at the tickle of those big lips so gently nibbling her skin.

"He was in a stock trailer that rolled down an incline during a storm. He was the only survivor of four." Sophie listened as he related how Pana had nearly killed Cole's daughter last year when she got under his feet during a storm. "It wasn't intentional aggression," Tucker explained. "It was the storm and a case of Birdie being in the wrong place at the wrong time. Pana's doing better, aren't you boy?" He patted the horse's neck. "He's learning to leave the past behind."

Sophie's shoulders sagged a bit. The reassurance in Tucker's voice made it seem like maybe he was comforting her and not Pana. Which was ridiculous, because how could he know the twisty path she'd been walking on? Before she could lament any more, he thrust the reins in her hands. She took them on reaction.

"What? He's dangerous!" She moved to drop the reins, but Tucker put a hand over hers and closed her fingers.

"You could smash this horse between a T-rex and an atom bomb and he'd stand here looking lazy and stupid just like he is right now. Unless there's a storm. Or you try to put him in a trailer. Or ride him." He grinned like he'd just told a joke as he walked to the far side of the pen.

Sophie called after him. "Then why do I have to hold onto him?"

"Because you look sexy when you squirm." Tucker picked something up and came back over, smirking lightheartedly when he saw how stiffly she was standing. With quick movements, Tucker unhooked the bridle from Pana's head and let it fall to the ground. Pana snorted, tossed his head. Before she could back up, Tucker took her left hand and placed it on Pana's big, round jaw. A flicker of panic made her want to swivel away, but his palm was warm and rough where it pressed into her skin, giving her a tremble. Slowly,

Tucker moved their hands so her fingers ran over Pana's silky hide.

"He likes this after you take the halter off. Don't ya, pain in the ass?" Pretty soon, Tucker had both of her hands in his, ran them over Pana's face and ears. The horse leaned into their touch with soft, pleased grunts. Sophie was amazed how he relished the attention, even begged for more by pressing into her hands. All that power, all that muscle and angst was reduced to a puddle with some simple, affectionate attention. And love. Because Tucker was giving this huge animal love, there was no doubt, just to help him have a better life.

Sophie broke free of Tucker's touch, relieved when he stepped back to allow her to move away from Pana. The horse snorted and trotted away, leaving Tucker to pick up the bridle and Sophie to try and gather her storm of emotions.

"We need to talk, Tucker."

"Yeah?"

Tucker fiddled with a strap on the bridle and she didn't push to fill the silence that stretched between them. If only they could have met another time…a couple years from now, after she had her life back on track. A breeze ruffled her bangs, prompting her to look up at the mountain peaks that tipped the sun and the brilliant shades of green all around her. She glanced at the dirt on her hands from petting the horse—dirt that at one time would have made her run to the nearest sink. Right now, it was a reminder that she was firmly present in this moment, in this place.

Tucker slung the bridle over his shoulder. "Well, since I'm so good at it, three guesses on the topic."

"Tucker…"

"You broke a fingernail?" He cocked his head with a teasing grin. "No? Okay. You were thinking about your… puppy that died when you were in the fourth grade, and it made you sad."

She scoffed. "I never had a puppy."

"Yeah, I imagine not. Then that only leaves one topic that could put such a sour look on your face." He turned his back to grab a little wooden box with brushes and other horse things peeking out of it. "Must be a man involved."

He turned back to her, one hand running over his middle. "Am I right?"

"Yes, but there's no prize this time." She'd wanted that to come out jokingly, but it fell flat.

He cleared his throat as he approached the fence. "I'm getting that impression." Tucker set down the things and rested an elbow on the rail, facing her. There seemed to be more he wanted to say, so she waited, but he didn't go on, so she stared at her feet a moment, studying the grime on the tips of her flats and realizing she'd need more rugged footwear if she was going to hang out at the ranch much longer.

Stupid thought.

"You know, it's going to sound so lame and cliché, but I have a lot going on right now…"

"That's a cop-out Sophie," Tucker interrupted. He pulled a toothpick from his back pocket and put it between his teeth. It bobbed up and down, hugged tightly by those sensual lips. "And you're not a cop-out kind of girl."

"You want me to explain the personal details of my life to you?" It was too personal, too intimate to share her mother's condition and her family drama with him. No, that would be getting closer, letting him in more. A complete contrast to what she needed to do. "Well, I can't."

"I figured there were a lot of things I couldn't do, too, and here I am doing them."

She took the bait, against her better judgment. "Like what?"

He grinned around the toothpick, though the expression didn't meet his eyes. "I don't figure it matters much, considering you're here to tell me we can't see each other anymore. Did I guess that right, too?" The sarcastic edge to his voice was soft, but not hidden and it cut her regardless.

"Look, I don't know how to integrate anything else into my life right now. It's not fair to you, Tucker."

Tucker pushed away from the fence and looked up at the sky as his hands found his hips. The smooth, masculine planes of his cheekbones were highlighted in shadow as a cloud moved over the sun, and gave his facial structure a cut, rugged deliciousness. "I've learned to live with not fair, Sophie. But I've also learned that you can't take what's not there. Are you saying there's nothing inside of you for me?"

This tender side of him was an element she hadn't yet seen. The dominant, sexy side, the toughness, the commanding presence and the stubborn anger were the pieces that made up the cowboy she knew. But this…he was almost laying his heart on the line, maybe was in the only way he knew how, and it reminded her how much she still didn't know about this man. The softness gutted her.

She shook her head. "I'm not saying that." It was just impossible to work around the part of her heart that was singularly beating for her mother. That was a love that couldn't be moved or added to right now.

Tucker's hand slid along the rail as if he might touch her leg. His fingers came within an inch of her knee, but he didn't reach out any more. If he did touch her, she'd probably melt right off the fence and beg him for a kiss like he'd given her last night. That kiss, and his confession, had left her dazed the rest of her shift. How she'd both muddled through and warded off Pasha's questions was a miracle.

The slice of her cell phone's ringtone broke the silence. Tucker took a quick step back as if the sound had startled him. Jumping down, Sophie grabbed the cell from her pocket, noting Carla's number on the screen. With one look at Tucker, she squeezed through the fence rails and answered the call, walking slowly back toward the ranch, with the sensation that she was somehow in deeper with Tucker now than she'd been before.

Chapter Seventeen

A package waited for Sophie when she walked behind the bar to get her apron the next night. A silver box with a gorgeous turquoise silk bow on the top sported a little card with her name.

"That's a Moonbeam box!" Bren grabbed it from Sophie's hands and regarded it like a priceless treasure a moment before sniffing it. She sighed with her eyes closed. "See, it even has the store smell." Sophie reached for the box. Bren gave it over after a short tug-of-war. Cautiously, Sophie sniffed the box, not sure what she was expecting. It smelled like vanilla—the good kind made with expensive, multi-note bourbon with a dark draw and sweet, caramelized undertone.

Her fingertips tingled as she traced the ribbon. "What's Moonbeam?"

"The most expensive boutique in Montana, that's what." Pasha trailed her fingers dreamily over the box before leaning down to take a long whiff. "Who the hell did you impress the other night with that dance of yours?"

Sophie shrugged, set the box down, and began tying on

her apron. Two nights had passed since her stint on stage, and with the amount of men who had been thrusting money at her, there was no telling who might have sent it. Sophie's stomach did an uncomfortable flippy thing. The thought that some random stranger from the bar last night may have gotten her a gift sat about as comfortably as a rotten steak.

Bren grabbed her arms. "Are you nuts? Why are you waiting to open it?"

"I…don't know. I just…" She hadn't taken a dime offered to her that night, except for the two hundred Dave had paid her for her "performance," and she didn't want anything else.

Bren and Pasha slid the box into Sophie's hands at the same time. "Open the damn box!"

Fred Decorta, the bartender, stopped drying glasses as he wandered over. "Yeah, open the box. I've smelled that damn thing for hours and it's making me hungry. Smells like candy." He leaned heavily tattooed forearms on the bar and waited, the large silver ring piercings in his eyebrows bobbling with expectantly arched brows.

Sophie pulled the ribbon slowly. "You know who dropped this off?"

Fred frowned with a chuckle. "A man's gotta keep his word, Sophie, so don't even ask." Bren clapped her hands with an excited hurry-up gesture as the ribbon fell away and Sophie lifted the cover. Filmy white tissue lay neatly tucked over the opening. Sophie peeled it back, stopped just before revealing what was inside. Looking at Bren, she shrugged and put the tissue back down. "Maybe I'll open it later."

Bren grabbed her wrist. "I'll kill you. I swear. I'll carve you into little pieces and feed them to my rodeo bull!" Still looking at Bren with a smarmy smile, Sophie pulled back the tissue. Even Fred gasped. A carefully folded silver-gray shirt lay in beautiful contrast to the white tissue. The V-neck top was trimmed in lace and a smattering of brilliant sequins and tiny crystal beads that shimmered like a disco ball in the bar lights. Sophie looped her fingers through the satin spaghetti straps and lifted the tank top. The hem had the same bead and lace trim. The fabric was slinky, shiny, and smooth, and felt ridiculously expensive.

Pasha drew an admiring breath. "This is the shirt from the display window. Jesus, Sophie, it costs two hundred and twenty-five dollars!" The straps slipped from Sophie's fingers and the shirt floated back into the box.

"What?"

"Is there a card?" Bren gave an accusing glance at Fred, who looked away with a little whistle. Unable to laugh because her lips were numb, Sophie searched the box and found a small bi-fold card at the bottom. Heart racing, she flipped it open. The handwriting was neat and masculine.

In case you get tired of that shirt you're wearing right now.

She glanced down at her uniform shirt, knowing immediately who'd sent it. "Son of a bitch!" The words sputtered out before she could stop them. Sweet warmth swirled with irate anger that Tucker would get her something so beautiful and expensive. Even after their conversation yesterday in the corral, he'd still done this. To prove a point, she was sure—to remind her that he didn't approve of her working here. Like his approval was any more important to her than it had been before. God, she needed a minute to let her anger at his impetuousness brew a little. Bastard! The look of realization blossomed on Pasha's face. First a scowl and then a smile. Then a bigger smile as she mouthed the word, "whoa."

Sophie held the shirt against her chest, petting the silky fabric with reluctant fingers. She folded it back into the box and slid it back under the bar as the doors opened and people began to filter in.

Pasha grabbed her arm. "Was that from Tucker?"

"Unfortunately, yes."

Pasha turned Sophie to face her. "I've known Tucker a long time, Sophie. He's the biggest bachelor around here, and you can ask anyone—he doesn't do something like this."

Considering what Pasha had said about his playing status the other day, this just added a layer of curiosity. "Like what?"

"Gifts, or seeing the same woman more than once. Being jealous, the way he was the other night. You're in unchartered Tucker Haywood territory here, and I gotta admit, I'm jealous as hell."

Fred sided up to them, all too eager to jump in on the gossip. He cracked a can of Sprite and took a drink. "Explains why he's been hanging around. Haven't seen the boy in what, eight…maybe nine months and all of a sudden, he's back…" Fred winked.

"Yeah, he's pretty protective." Pasha tapped her chin with her finger and nodded at Fred. "Last year, his sister-in-law, Rylan came in here and some punk hit on her. She broke his nose and got away from him, but that didn't stop Tucker from tracking that kid down in here a few days later and putting the fear of God in him."

Fred gave an approving nod. "Didn't lay a finger on that fratty bratty to get his point across. Didn't have to." Fred took another drink, more slowly this time. "You know, Sophie, he keeps his family close. He wouldn't be watching after you like this unless he…"

That was exactly what she was afraid of. "Don't say it!" Sophie grabbed a couple pens from beneath the bar and shoved them in her apron pocket. A clench of suffocation grabbed her throat, making it hard to swallow. The gift and his continual presence in the bar were his way of making his point over his dislike of her working here. He was being stubborn in her rejection, that's all. Sophie pounded down the lump in her throat and turned away, eager to get to work and forget the little vanilla-smelling box under the bar. She was only filling in until eight and the time passed in a whirlwind of chatter, drink, and food orders and raunchy banter, but none of it took her mind off that damn shirt. Tucker was an arrogant bastard, and the more she thought about it, the more pissed she got.

She made another round through her circle of tables, noticing from the corner of her eye that the last table, which had been empty, was now occupied. It only took a nanosecond and a double flip of her heart to know it was Tucker. He was slouched in the chair; legs spread wide, arms behind his head with the top buttons on his shirt undone. He was watching her. A wave of lightheadedness washed over her, an impact, Sophie grumbled, from seeing him here. Again. She set her jaw and strode over, weaving through the crowd with the sickly realization that she wasn't completely unhappy to see him. All sprawled out in the chair, his hard-cut chest outlined by the thin shirt, strong thighs snuggled into perfectly worn Wranglers, he was deliciousness wrapped up in extra arrogance.

A wicked smile turned his mouth into a delectable confection as she approached. The irritating toothpick flit from one side of his mouth the other as his smile grew. With a steady smile, Sophie stepped right between his wide-spread legs and gripped his thighs with her hands, though her insides were shaking. He was warm under her hands. And firm. Too damn firm, reminding her it had been days since he'd touched her—really, really touched her.

"Hey, Fifi." Tucker set the chair down on all four legs. She leaned in, the deep, rich notes of his scent wrapping around her. The Moonbeam box had nothing on Tucker. God, he smelled good. A nip of lightheadedness returning, she leaned in just a little more, tempted to lick his neck and sample skin she knew tasted as good as it smelled. It would be warm and wicked like sin on her tongue.

It would be dancing with poison.

Sophie grabbed the toothpick from his lips. "Here again, Tucker? I believe this constitutes stalking."

"Ouch!" He put a hand over his heart. The back of one hand slid along her waist and over her hip. Sophie couldn't hold back a shudder before she stopped his hand. She wanted to be bitter about the shirt, but it wouldn't develop. She'd never been pursued before, and this seemed a lot like being chased. It was sweet, despite her inability to act on his attention. As Tucker's hands moved to take her hips between them, Sophie let herself enjoy this chase, just a little. Just right now, and then, it was back to warding him off.

Biting back desire, she smiled sweetly. "Thank you for the shirt. It's beautiful." She wanted to ask if he minded if she returned it and kept the money, just to rattle him. "Just so you know, I like how my boobs look in this Tit for Tap shirt. But thanks anyway." She shoved the toothpick back between his lips and moved to back out of his legs. Tucker's hands gripped her hips and stopped her tight.

"That's not a proper thank you, Sophie."

• • •

He didn't know why he bought that damn shirt. Probably because he'd pictured her wearing it without a bra, the thin fabric molding her perfect breasts in a clingy hug while her nipples tried to poke through. And then he remembered how men had tried to touch her the other night and rage made him want to wrap her in a sheet and duct tape it tight so no part of her was accessible. Except to him, of course.

There'd been a moment when male pride drove him to buy that shirt, the kind that would show Sophie he could take care of her. It was a reflection of his money, one he wasn't comfortable with and had never used to his advantage with women before, but plunking down a couple hundred like it was spare change to get her something pretty had made him feel…nice. If it was money that was holding her back, then, she could just lay those problems right in his palms and he'd take care of it.

Even as he thought about it now, his skin prickled at simply throwing money down for a woman. It was serious, this conflict in him. But hell, Sophie cut through his brain like a strobe light, always there, flashing her pretty face into instant recall, the image of her swaying, dancing body on constant replay. He missed her. He wanted her to go away. He wanted to pull her closer and, holy hell, he wanted her next to him every day, and every night, and he had no earthly idea how to begin to process that. In the very rare moments he'd allowed himself to dream about a relationship, maybe even a family of his own, it had never been more real or visceral than when Sophie had fallen at his feet in a near-puking heap of beautiful.

Her soft hips leaning into his palms were sweet torture. Tucker dug his fingers into the rise of her ass and pulled her in until her thighs met the juncture of his. She gasped, but she didn't pull away. He walked his hands up her hips, up her waist to her ribs and pulled her down while he rose up and sat straighter in the chair. He'd ached for her for days, and as his cock stirred now, he was painfully reminded of how much he'd missed having her close.

Tucker moved her to the side so he could press his legs together, and then pulled her on top, facing him, her thighs straddling his. His fingers dug into her hips, shamelessly pulling her center over the bulge in his jeans. Her quick intake of breath fueled him. They were in the corner, covered in shadow that gave them a filmy sense of cover. He could go a little further; no one would see. Hell, he didn't give a shit if they did. Tucker placed his lips on her neck, sucking and nibbling his way to the curve of her collarbone.

"I could take you right here, Fifi." He pulled her down harder against his crotch. "Just like this, baby. Hot and fast."

She sucked in a tight breath, involuntarily moving her hips against him. "Just bury your face in my shoulder when you come, and no one will know."

Her lips met his with a soft gasp and Tucker knew this was it, this was falling, but it didn't feel like he imagined it would. It hurt deep and it pulsed with a frantic beat from the fear that she might not be falling too.

"Jesus, Tucker." Her breathy voice didn't hold a lick of dissuasion, but as his palms moved to take her breasts, Sophie put her hands on his ribs and pushed back. He steadied her as she slipped off him, his breath coming fast and hard.

"Quit this damn bar, Fifi. Come back to Paint River with me." His voice was desperate, but he didn't care. That statement was open-ended and he wasn't even sure what he was asking her or what he was offering. He only knew he *needed* something and it involved her.

Her chest heaved. "I can't."

"You don't need this job."

She took his face with her hands, letting her thumbs linger on his cheekbones for a moment before she jerked away. "I do! I have obligations, Tucker. You have no idea…"

"Then *tell* me." Tucker lowered his voice as he pulled her down onto one thigh, and wrapped his arms around her waist. People were getting closer to their corner as they milled around. "Tell me why."

She checked her watch right before reaching behind her back and untying her apron. Then, she reached for his hand. "How about if I show you instead?"

• • •

Tucker pressed his heels into the cement walkway as Sophie opened the door. She walked through and glanced back at him, but he couldn't move. Why the hell had she brought him to a convalescent home? The thought that maybe Sophie finally snapped and broke Carla's neck passed through his mind, but he shrugged off the sarcasm, feeling there was something much more serious at work here. Sophie had put a thin blue cardigan over her Tit for Tap shirt, and let her hair down. She looked soft and vulnerable. The veil of sadness he'd seen on her face now and then returned. He had the sinking feeling he was about to meet the source.

"Visiting hours are over in thirty minutes, so come on."

He followed her up two short flights of stairs and through a pair of stained glass doors. A long desk waited just inside. A nurse looked up, her lips spreading into a surprised smile.

"Sophie! This is kind of late for you." Her voice was soothing and warm. The nurse rose from her chair and touched Sophie's hand across the desk. Tucker pulled at his shirt, smoothed it.

"May I see her?" Sophie picked up a pen and signed her name on a sheet of paper attached to a clipboard. The nurse nodded and waved them down the hall. Sophie led him to the last door on the left and opened it. He took off his hat, wishing he could beat his nerves with it. Hospitals and nursing homes meant sick people. Sick people caused their loved ones to have emotions. Tucker didn't want Sophie to have emotions, not bad ones anyway. Her anger he could handle. Her tears, not so much.

The room was dimly lit and sparsely furnished. A large armoire sat against the far wall, a flat screen TV next to it. There was a writing desk, a dresser, and two armchairs. In the middle of it all was a bed with silver side rails pulled up high. Sophie leaned over and spoke softly.

Tense to the point of nausea, Tucker stepped up behind

Sophie. His fingers went numb, the hat nearly falling from his grip when he saw the frail woman lying like a skeletal heap on the mattress. A thin sheet and cable knit blanket were pulled to her waist. Her chest rose and fell slowly beneath a floral nightgown, the bones of her sternum and ribs highlighted where the fabric had settled in-between them. Her head rested on a pillow, and a soft restraint was strapped across her forehead and connected behind the mattress to hold her head in place. A quick glance showed similar restraints across her chest. Sophie picked up the woman's left hand and brought it lovingly to her cheek.

"Tucker, I'd like you to meet my mother, Violet." Sophie kissed her mother's fragile hand and Tucker dropped his hat. He was glad when Sophie started to talk to her mother in hushed tones so he didn't have to attempt a response. Then she looked over her shoulder at him and smiled.

"Mom, this is my friend Tucker." Sad joy filled Sophie's smile. The inside of Tucker's chest swelled about three sizes. He slid his fingertips into the front pockets of his jeans, careful not to touch the bed rail, as he looked a little closer at Violet. Sophie's mother. He wanted to ask how…why, but didn't know if he should speak about Violet in front of her. Sophie's knowing smile reassured him, but not much. She turned and pulled a chair over for him. Taking the railing down, Sophie sat in her own chair and leaned her elbows on the mattress with Violet's hand between her own.

Tucker sat motionless as Sophie told him how Violet came to be injured, and about the woman, the mother, she'd been before the accident. Her voice rose between thick and condensed to light as she walked him down an abbreviated memory lane. When she stopped talking, he felt like he'd just run into a brick wall; he'd been hanging on her every word.

Sophie put a hand on her mom's stomach and laid her head on the mattress so her forehead rested against Violet's hip. For long moments, Sophie lay that way, almost like she'd forgotten he was in the room. Her fingers traced little circles and lines over the blanket. Violet lay still, eyes shut, mouth gaped, bony chest rising and falling, without any acknowledgement of her daughter's touch. Despite his discomfort at being in a place filled with emotions and the hint of death, he didn't feel like a stranger in the room. His blood pounded with an innate sadness for Sophie and the pain she held so tightly inside. He wanted to touch her, to give her some comfort, but seriously doubted the touch of his hand would do it. Tucker's fingers uncurled and fisted again as if they agreed.

It was a little twisted how much Sophie was struggling to let her mom die, while he struggled to let his live in the new life she'd chosen, with a new man.

Cold shivers dumped over his body like ice water. She straightened in her chair, looping her hair with one hand and pulling it over her shoulder. "So…now you see why I do what I do." She shifted in her chair to face him. Tucker's skin was tight and cold, his head throbbing. "It's…expensive here. I need to support her, make sure she's provided for in this place. Do you understand now?"

He forced himself to meet her eyes. Speaking would be useless; words would be a nonsensical mess thanks to his thick tongue. Just then the door opened and the nurse stepped in.

"Sophie, can I see you for a minute?" Sophie rose and met the nurse by the door. Tucker couldn't form a coherent thought while looking at Violet lying there like breathing death. Violet's breath hitched and sputtered, startling him. Little foamy bubbles pooled from the corner of her mouth and trickled down her chin. She sputtered softly again and her chest slowed. Jerking, Tucker grabbed a tissue from the nightstand and leaned closer. The tissue hovered over the foam. Instead of body warmth against his wrist, cool air wafted from Violet's frail body. The shape of her eyes and her straight nose with the blunt tip was familiar. Tucker bet if Violet could smile, he'd see two beautiful dimples that matched her daughter's. A small smile passed his lips as he wiped the spittle from Violet's mouth.

It could easily be Maeve lying here. He could be looking down on his own mother, watching her vitality and strength fading away into the night. The door opened and shut, Sophie walked back over. She ran her fingers through her mom's hair and placed a kiss on her cheek. Breath stuck behind Tucker's Adam's apple at the absolute grief on Sophie's face. She looked down when she turned to him.

"I'm going to hang out here for a little bit. Thank you for coming to meet her." That she'd shared this precious part of her life with him was more of a privilege than Tucker felt he deserved. Her absolute devotion to her mother brought him to his knees. All the pieces fell into place now, completing the puzzle of the constant challenge that was Sophie's life. Something unnamable inside him snapped.

Tucker still didn't trust himself to speak. So he squeezed her shoulder and turned to leave as Sophie sat down. Her soft voice was filled with tears that cut Tucker to the bone.

"I love you, Mom."

Sophie's words followed him out. Shutting the door, he leaned against it for just a moment to collect the uncomfortable shivers picking at his skin and throw them away. The nurse gave him a small, sympathetic smile. With a nod, Tucker turned to walk down the hall, paused. Then, he turned, and without a second thought, walked back to the nurse's desk.

Chapter Eighteen

So much for self control.

Tucker had promised himself he wasn't going to the Tit to see Sophie again, but he'd had his fingers crossed so it didn't count. Something profound had happened between them at the convalescent home yesterday. Maybe it was more on his part than hers, he didn't know. All Tucker knew for sure was that he'd crossed a line he'd promised himself never to step over again—and he'd done something to solidify the way he cared for Sophie—something he wasn't sure he should tell her about. He still couldn't believe he'd done, it though he didn't regret it for a second.

As he watched Sophie preparing the stage for tonight's band, Tucker did regret that he still couldn't completely rationalize his feelings for her. He cared, yeah. And it terrified the hell out of him. Because he wasn't completely convinced that he could be the man she'd need, that he wouldn't make her turn away.

But before he could ponder that further, a man made his way through the crowd to stand by the stage, and had no qualms about openly gawking at Sophie. It only took a second for recognition to hit Tucker. He knew that portly outline well. Too well. Blaise Lampe had always been a cow with a bull's mean streak.

Tucker sat a little straighter in his chair and gripped his beer glass so hard his knuckles cracked. He'd seen Jewel's father here and there in passing, in the years since Blaise had forbid his daughter from marrying Tucker. Their last face-to-face meeting had left him marinating in the belief that he'd never be good enough. And all these years, he'd believed it. Except that Sophie was making him rethink that some.

And by the look on Blaise's face, Sophie was giving him thoughts, too. Thoughts Tucker would love nothing more than to shake out of the older man's head. Taking his beer, Tucker forced a slow, controlled pace as he strode up next to Blaise and nonchalantly took a sip. The older man wobbled a bit, his eyes following Sophie as she walked back and forth across the stage. A tickle of satisfaction made Tucker smirk at just how fat and bald Blaise had gotten in the past few years.

Tucker took another drink. "She sure looks nice, huh?"

Blaise didn't look at him. Just smiled deep and sloppy, and took a drink from his beer. "Oh yeah."

Tucker bit back the need for violence. He'd been pushed between his father's temper and Blaise's condemnation like a ping pong ball. Tucker blinked fast with the realization of just how much anger he'd been holding onto because of that. Really, he'd known it was there, but right now, for the first time, the force of it was burning him inside. His dad might be gone, but Blaise was standing right in front of him. He forced down another drink. "Ummm hmmm."

Sophie walked to the far right corner of the stage. Blaise's eyes went with her, one elbow chicken-winging into Tucker's arm. "She looks like the type I could coax out back later. Money talks with chicks like her."

Tucker considered how much of a beating he could lay down before the cops got here. "Cheating on your wife, Lampe? I always knew you and my dad had something in common." Tucker braced his feet as Blaise turned. The older man looked Tucker up and down with choppy tilts of his chin and a sarcastic huff. Tucker smirked as the older man cranked his neck to look up at him. He'd forgotten Blaise was a good three inches shorter than him.

"Figures you'd be bar slumming, Haywood."

Just then, Sophie turned their way. Eyes squinting against the light, she spotted Tucker and smiled. Her small acknowledgement warmed him. What he felt for Sophie couldn't compare to anything from his past and nothing in his future would ever hold a flame to it. There would never be another Sophie, but standing here next to Blaise, Tucker wasn't convinced he deserved her any more than he'd deserved Jewel.

"She married a cardiologist." Blaise burped and gave a slow, wicked smile. "That's a *heart* doctor." Tucker watched Sophie's movements on the stage to keep his anger in check. Blaise dove in with gusto. "Two great kids. You know, she cried over you for…maybe a day or two. Didn't take her long to…to realize she could do better."

Tucker took another swig just to keep himself in check. If Blaise had quit ogling Sophie, he might have been able to just walk away. But no, the man wagged his eyebrows and licked his bottom lip in her direction before making a slow glance back to Tucker. Now the fat bastard was just egging him on. And god damn it, he'd had messed with his woman once, and Tucker would go to hell before he'd let him get away with it again.

Tucker hoped like hell that Blaise's words were true— that Jewel was married to a heart doctor with two great kids and a great life. She deserved it. All of it. But this wasn't about her. After weathering emotions last night while imagining his own mother taking Violet Miller's place on that hospital bed, and trying to unravel his feelings for Sophie, Tucker's patience was unraveling in a hurry.

The emotions Lampe rekindled in him were both forbidden and welcome. Tucker had tried hard over the years to keep his quick anger at bay. He was good at walking away when he had to. But right now, he didn't want to. For years, he'd been the mini-Cooper Haywood who liked to brawl, was stubborn as a dead mule, and temperamental. He could live up to that reputation, no problem.

If Blaise wanted a fight, he'd have to do better than passive-aggressive dribble. Tucker never threw the first punch, but he wasn't afraid to follow up on one. He'd never had the opportunity to stand up for himself when Blaise had slung insults at him because he'd walked away to try and be the bigger man. The unburied anger in his blood said fuck being the bigger man.

He faced the older man with a lazy smirk. "You know as well as I do that Jewel sees my face when she's screwing him." It was a horrible thing to say. The bitter taste of bile rose in his throat as he spoke, but the words had the effect he'd hoped for.

Lampe swung first.

Tucker took the blow below his left cheek. The sting barely had a chance to hurt before he swung back, clocking Lampe between the eyes and driving him back against the stage. Sophie screamed, the crowd quieted.

Before Blaise could guard his face, Tucker hit him again. "That's for being a piece of shit and pretending otherwise." Blaise's hands came up palms out as Tucker drew his fist back again. Robby, the floor bouncer was there before Tucker could put his fist down. Tearing his glare from Blaise, he shrugged off Robby's grip on his shoulder. Good thing they knew each other well enough that Tucker could brush Robby off without consequence.

"Don't bother, Robby. I'm leaving. Just promise to make sure Sophie makes it to her car safe."

Tucker threw Sophie a glance over his shoulder. She stood frozen in place on the stage, watching him walk away. His heart fell. Robby cleared the crowd with the swipe of an arm as they walked to the bar. At the door, Robby patted Tucker on the shoulder.

"I'll walk her out for you, Tuck. And hey—we all saw Lampe swing first." Robby winked and shut the door. Alone on the sidewalk, Tucker stared at the door and bit his lower lip. Nothing about this felt anywhere near as satisfying as he'd believed it would. He'd lost his temper like Lampe wanted him to. Now that it was over, Tucker knew he hadn't really hurt Blaise. He'd proven him right.

• • •

Later that night, patrons had whispered about Tucker and Lampe's history, something about an almost engagement to Lampe's daughter. Blaise had been ogling her before the Tucker incident, but he'd never made a pass at her. Sophie figured that whatever set Tucker off had nothing to do with her, but had brought out his inner demon. And the more she thought about Tucker's almost engagement and almost wife, the worse the tension inside became.

For a man who'd sworn off relationships, he sure seemed to have a basketful of women outside his front door, her included. The longing her heart had for him was unlike anything she'd ever felt for anyone. Loving him wasn't a choice, it was like breathing, and when she let herself imagine the possibilities, Sophie wanted to breathe Tucker in until she couldn't inhale anymore.

Tucker conjured up so much more in her. She could easily take away the sex and still be content just to sit quietly with him, or watch him work. He made her want things. A family. A home. Roots. He made her want to leave the lights of the city behind for the brilliance of a Montana night sky.

Just when she'd thought there wasn't room in her life for him, for anyone else, suddenly there was. Maybe her heart had grown a little just for him. The timing was still off, her life was still uncertain, but maybe she could afford to hear him out completely. In a way, she owed him that much for the effort he'd been going through to let him know how he felt. Knowing he'd already been in love once, and had put himself out there again, for her, broke something inside her. Her resolve, her resolution to keep love at bay until it was "the right time."

What if there never was a right time?

Sophie showered and dressed in a pretty, sleeveless cream and pink floral dress she'd found at a second hand shop. It had a deep V-neck and nipped waist with a flowing skirt that hugged her hips and hung just above her knees. She added a brown leather belt and let her hair hang down wet. Tired of makeup, she added a little moisturizer and lip gloss and walked out into the mid-morning sun. Other guests were already up and about. She nodded to a few as she walked the drive from the cabins to the main house, then veered off to the right and headed down to the barns.

She had no idea where Tucker might be this time of day, but it was imperative that she find him. His days varied, he'd told her once, and with it being haying season, he often went back and forth between Paint River and Agate Falls. Knowing Tucker and Jaxon were often joined at the hip, she had a blossom of hope when she spotted Jaxon coming out of the horse barn. She called a greeting and he paused, giving her an appreciative look-over.

"Hell, Sophie. Country life is looking good on you."

She blushed. "Thanks. Any idea where I can find Tucker?"

Jaxon tipped his hat back a little and gave her a steady stare. She couldn't read his expression, but it was strong enough to give her a shiver. "Hayloft in that brown barn right there. Walk in, go up the ladder on your immediate right." With a nod, he wandered off, but not before a huge smile cracked his face. "Be warned," Jaxon called. "He's downright hostile today."

She swallowed down a flicker of anxiety and followed Jax's directions. Climbing a ladder wasn't what she had in mind when she'd put on this dress. Luckily her sandals didn't slide as she cleared the rungs and poked her head through the opening into the cavernous mow. Sunlight streamed into the space from the open loft door, but mounds of hay created blobs of darkness and shadow. Stepping into the mow, Sophie wiped her hands on her dress and picked her way carefully through the room.

"Tucker?" Little flecks of chaff danced in the streaming sunlight like nature's confetti. Loose hay crunched under her feet. Despite its size, the room was a little humid and warm.

"What the hell, Sophie?" Tucker stepped out from behind a stack of hay, his leather-clad fingers gripping a huge square bale by twine strings. He tossed the bale onto another stack like it weighed nothing. The squint in his eyes and hard line of his mouth might have been misread as exertion, but she wasn't fooled. He gave her a once over, his expression never changing.

"I needed to see you." Sophie rubbed her arms. Tucker turned and grabbed another bale.

"I've got work to do." He hauled another bale, lifting and throwing it effortlessly. His biceps bulged with the strenuous movement, his chest muscles contracting under the thin layer of his light brown Henley. Hatless, the deep brown waves of Tucker's hair shone red and gold in the sunlight.

"What happened last night?" Sophie crossed her arms tighter and followed him when he walked away. Tucker shook his head and swiped an irritated hand to dismiss her.

"Don't you have something to do, Sophie?"

His dismissal stung and this change in him was outright alarming. "I'm doing it."

"Let me be clear: go away." He pulled off his gloves and ran a bare forearm across his face. Grabbing a water bottle, Tucker downed half of it. Sophie blinked back the ache. Jaxon warned her and he hadn't been kidding. She'd hoped to find out what had spurred him to violence last night, but now she was a bit afraid to know. This Tucker didn't display an inch of the tenderness she'd seen in him when he'd helped her pet Pana. This Tucker was cut from a completely different cloth.

Taking a deep breath, Sophie steeled herself. "Tucker…"

He threw the bottle with a loud curse. Sophie jumped as water streaked over her shins. "What do you want from me, Sophie? Huh? You want an explanation for why I punched an old guy in the face?" He spread his arms wide with a sarcastic chuckle. "Because I'm an asshole. I am a *piece of shit* and you should run far, far away!"

He spun and walked near the gaping loft door. A rope, nearly twice the size of Tucker's wrist, hung down from the ceiling. He grabbed it and swung it forward. Sophie looked up to the sound of metal on metal as a steel pulley slid forward on an overhead track. Tucker guided the rope to a Y-shaped floor-to-ceiling beam and started looping it around.

Without thought, Sophie walked up behind him and put a hand on his shoulder. Tucker tensed under her touch. "I wouldn't run from you." Her voice was shaking, but not nearly as much as her insides were. Tucker turned slowly, his sleepy eyes heavy with dark emotion. He grabbed her wrist in one hand and held her for long seconds, his eyes boring into hers, his chest racing hers for each breath. Then he yanked her forward and Sophie forgot to breathe.

"You should," he growled.

Sophie's breath came out in little pants. "I don't want to. I don't want to go anywhere." *I'll stay with you. Just ask me to.*

"Forget what I said Sophie. I don't want you here—I don't need you here." Behind the pang his words gave her, Sophie called bullshit. She forced herself to call him on it, though she was feeling anything but brave.

"Liar."

"God fucking dammit!" Tucker cupped the back of her head and kissed her fiercely, his tongue doing sweet war with hers and claiming dominance. He leaned his back against the beam and hitched one leg slightly forward. With rough hands, he pulled her onto him so she straddled his waist. Inch after inch of flesh bared to the warm air as her skirt rode high around her thighs. Tucker owned her with one hand at the small of her back, the other at the base of her neck, and his lips on hers. And then he hitched her up a little more until her knees hit the beam and her sex rubbed against the waist of his jeans. Sudden and intense pleasure ripped through her as the rough denim of his jeans, and the cotton of her panties rubbed against her center.

Tucker's lips dipped to her neck. "You smell so damn good." He nuzzled the curve of her neck and nipped little tugs of flesh with his teeth. Exhaling deeply, Tucker moved his hips just a little, causing his trapped erection to rub against the center of her panties. Sophie shouted, one hand gripping his shoulder like she might fall. She had no idea how he was holding her up and moving like that without falling over. His hips thrust gently forward again, streaking a long draw of friction straight against her clit. Sparks danced behind her eyes.

"Tucker!" Her hands took on a frenzy of their own as she pulled his shirt from the tight waist of his jeans. Then he was kissing her again and moving his hips harder this time, giving unrelenting little rocks back and forth while one hand held her firmly against him. Pleasure hit her with a dizzying blow. Trying to hold back, wanting to hold back, Sophie arched her hips, intending to move away, but Tucker held her tight, grinding the hard length of his erection against her. Sparks returned in a full-on display of color and intensity as she settled over him.

Sophie slid her hands under Tucker's shirt. Warm, supple skin blanketed with soft hair covered hard mounds and ridges of muscle. She'd never really seen him naked, never really touched him and the craving to do both almost overwhelmed the pleasure fog in her brain. Living to thwart her, Tucker grabbed her hands and pulled them away.

He nipped her earlobe. "I could be buried so deep inside you right now." Tucker jetted his hips forward. Sensation ripped through her, sending her to the edge. She tried to slide her hands up his chest, kneading his soft flesh, the other itching to release his zipper and free him. Tucker stopped her hands with one of his.

"Let me touch you," she begged. Tucker moved her hands back down. Sophie curled her fingers as if her nails against his skin would slow down the loss of contact. "I want to touch you." She leaned her forehead into his shoulder when his cock rubbed against her fast, once, twice, three times. "Please…Tucker, please!" she didn't know what she was begging for anymore.

"You're so damn wet. I can feel it through my jeans." Tucker groaned and moved in steady rhythm. Sophie grabbed his shoulders, hung on as her orgasm built fast and hard. He arched his back and rubbed against her almost violently, pulling her down so the friction caused pleasure-pain that catapulted her into full-blown release. Sophie screamed against the bare curve of his neck, pressing against him as hard and as closely as possible. The jerky movements of Tucker's breathing caused ripples through her pelvis that milked the pleasure until she was completely drained.

Tucker's arms trembled as he lowered her. Sophie leaned in to kiss him as her fingers let loose the button and zipper on his jeans. Not waiting, not giving him a chance to react, she gripped his cock in one hand and opened the fly of his jeans as far as it would go. Bastard wouldn't let her touch him so now she'd leave him defenseless.

. . .

Her hand on his cock felt incredible, but he wanted to be buried inside Sophie's hot body more than anything. And he wanted it right now. She stroked him with a soft, slow glide and he allowed the pleasure to creep from his balls to his scalp. Closing his eyes for just a second, Tucker reached to pull her hand away. But Sophie dropped to her knees before he could react. Startled, Tucker looked down at the same time she took his dick in her mouth.

"Fuck!" His fingers found her hair on instinct, winding in it and holding her closer while his heart screamed that he pull her away. No touching, it was too intimate. This was firmly included in that rule. Sophie's slick mouth took him in, her lips stretching around his width, a deep groan of satisfaction rumbling against the tip as she took all of him. His dick hit the back of her throat. Tucker bit his lower lip with the force of the pleasure. Stupid, stupid rule.

Sophie's teeth scraped him lightly as she pulled back, sending shocks of electricity into his thighs. "God, do it again." She did. Again and again, until the pressure built and hovered on the brink of explosion. His entire body was on fire. He wanted to…he shouldn't…not like this.

Tucker pulled back on her hair at the same time he helplessly thrust into her mouth. "Sophie!" his voice was desperate for her to pull back, desperate for her to continue. She gripped his hips firmly in response, pulling him in and sliding back, only to pull him in again.

Then she clamped down with her palate, curving her tongue firmly under his cock as she slid him out in a long, tight stroke. Little sounds of suction accompanied her soft little moans of pleasure. He gripped her hair tight and pushed back in, the wet slide of her tongue pushing him over. He came hard and she took it all, holding him like this is exactly what she wanted.

He leaned his head back against the beam. Blood rushed in his ears, the room spun mercilessly. Fingers of pleasure raced up and down his flesh, pulling every nerve into an ecstasy-fueled mind trip. His right arm ached. Looking over, Tucker realized he'd grabbed a hold of the end of the rope and it looped several times around his wrist. Sophie's body slid along the length of his and Tucker wrapped her in his arm, his chin lolling over to rest on the top of her head as he freed himself. Her face burrowed into his neck as she gripped his ribs and held him back.

For a moment, the panic and anger he'd been holding inside passed. For just a second, everything felt normal. Sophie in his arms. His body filled with pleasure from connecting with the person who was just right for him. His other half. Tucker tipped her chin and looked down into Sophie's face. Her expression of contentment and soft satisfaction robbed his momentary peace away. She shouldn't be looking at him like that, and he shouldn't have allowed what just happened.

She was already too close to his heart. But he'd proven to himself last night why he couldn't ask her to stay. He'd completely lost the grip on his anger, let it control him, consume him. Warranted or not, that wasn't the man he wanted to be. That wasn't the kind of man Sophie deserved. Closing his eyes to break the visual of her beautiful face, Tucker set Sophie away from him and righted his jeans.

"Tell me" she said. Sophie smoothed the front of her dress. He didn't miss how her hands shook. Tucker looked away from her waist, pretended to be adjusting his belt.

"What?"

She reached for him. "Tell me that you feel something for me." The words were heavy and raw. Tucker's chest clenched hard. Last night pushed him over the edge—immersed him in his own fears of never being good enough for Sophie. Jesus, he'd never expected to be here, in the position to love or push it away again. He could tell her the truth or he could do the right thing, and set her free.

"I don't. You're a nice girl, Sophie." A nice girl who had him completely. But he couldn't have it. "But this has gone too far." Sunlight rippled between them, highlighting the confusion and hurt in Sophie's eyes. She blinked softly, her brow furrowed as if sorting out what he'd said. It took all of Tucker's strength not to start ripping the hay loft apart.

"Bastard," she uttered, before spinning away from him. She didn't turn away quickly enough though. He'd seen the shimmer of tears. Tucker's hands fell to his sides, his voice a whisper he didn't intend for her to hear.

"I know."

Sophie paused for a heartbeat, and he knew she'd heard him before she kept on walking. Her head disappeared below the floor as she descended the ladder. Tucker leaned against the beam, pinching the bridge of his nose with his fingers, fighting the urge to follow his heart.

Chapter Nineteen

Sophie walked past Carla with a paper grocery bag in each arm, ignoring the shocked expression on her sister's face. When Carla called, asking her to come over to discuss "matters," Sophie figured she'd force Carla into a baking lesson.

"She never taught me how to make pie." She dropped the bags onto the kitchen counter. Carla came up behind her, arms crossed. Sophie began taking items from the bags, shoving them where ever she could find room on the marble countertop. "I don't even know if he likes apple or peach or blueberry, so I…I just got it all."

"What are you doing?" Carla barked. "I just cleaned my kitchen!"

Sophie threw her a look over a shoulder. "Apparently you can't just put flour and milk and eggs into a bowl and mix it all up and get pie crust." Her voice grew thick. "No, no, there's a *technique*, according to this cookbook I read in the checkout line. Did you know there's a *technique*?" Sophie didn't even know why she was worried about it. Seriously, making pie for a man who'd basically given her the old "screw and toss" was ridiculous.

Carla's voice softened. "Honey, there isn't milk or eggs in pie crust."

"Well I suppose I would know that if she ever taught us how to fucking cook! Right?" Sophie slammed a container of eggs down. A fierce cracking sound exploded on impact. "I mean, all I want to do is make the man a…a pie and it's not like I can go to Mom and just ask her how to do it…"

Carla's soft touch on her arm made Sophie freeze. Her sister's face held a tenderness Sophie didn't know Carla was capable of. "Sophie, what's this about?"

Sophie rooted her eyes into Carla's, unable to move save for the tears that rolled hot and wet down her cheeks. She felt them burn and moisten her skin, pooling into the neckline of her shirt, but she didn't care. Carla's breathing increased, her fingers tightening over Sophie's arm. Everything felt numb, from her lower lip to her ankles—her muscles weak and suddenly useless as she slid down against the lower cabinets until her butt hit the floor with a thud.

What was this about? Maybe as a good-bye gesture for Tucker. Maybe as a way to prove to him that she could be more than a city girl and make a damn pie. When she'd woken up with her emotions throbbing, her hands needed something to do to keep her heart from breaking, and apple, peach, or strawberry was the first thing that came to mind. And this was one of those times when a woman needed her mother, to explain how to handle an ornery man with his heels dug in the wrong direction, how to stop her heart from hurting so bad.

Her voice trembled, thick with tears. "I just…I need her."

"Oh, Sophie, honey." Carla squatted down, both hands gripping Sophie's arm.

Sophie shook her head as pounding disequilibrium rocketed through her. She was far away-far, far away. "I'm in love with him and I just want to make him a pie. And I need her, Carla. I need her to tell me what to do." And then Carla's arms were around her, holding her in a sisterly embrace Sophie couldn't begin to register. She stared at the base of Carla's stainless steel refrigerator, noting a crayon peeked out from under the grate and a small dust bunny huddled off to one side.

"I *need* her." Her voice repeated, though it sounded distant and detached. Like her mother would be if she raced to her bedside and pleaded for her to come back to them, to be the mother she wasn't nearly ready to let go of. Sophie leaned into Carla, grabbing her sleeve with one hand like she could hang on and make the pain inside go away.

Carla pulled back just a little. "Who are you in love with?"

"What?" Sophie sniffed. Suddenly realizing she was actually hugging her *sister*, Sophie leaned back and covered her mouth with the back of her hand. Carla wiped at her eyes and rocked on her heels.

"You said, 'I'm in love with him.' So, who is it? And when did you meet someone since you've been here?"

"I did not."

"Yes, you did. Wait…the cowboy from the carnival?" Carla's eyes went huge with a twinkle. "Him?"

Sophie shook her head, feeling some of the dread inside her lift. Yeah, it was him all right. "Just a guy who likes pie."

Carla rose with a sigh. "You really want to learn how to make pie?"

"Yeah." Because her time at the ranch was coming to an end, and she didn't want to leave things like this between her and Tucker. It was silly, but a pie would be a good parting gesture.

Carla reached into a high cupboard and pulled out two wine glasses. After a moment's consideration, she pulled a bottle of sweet Moscato from the wine rack. "Fine, but you clean the mess," Carla grabbed a wine corker and shook it in Sophie's direction. "And you don't say a word about how many glasses of wine it takes me to put up with you. Deal?"

"Only if you have another bottle so I can do the same."

Carla huffed with a smile, popped the bottle, and poured. Then she sat on the floor next to Sophie and handed her a glass. The sipped in silence as Sophie struggled to get the last bit of her emotions under control.

"You know, I always saw Mom as mine. Then you came along, little Miss Perfect, never doing anything wrong, and I saw how she looked at you—how proud she was of her perfect daughter." Carla stared blankly at the refrigerator. "It was hard living in your shadow, Sophie."

Sophie set her wine glass down with a clink on the flagstone floor. "I know."

"When she got hurt, the responsibility of her care fell completely on me. At least, that's how it felt, but it's not true." Their eyes met and a fresh sob bubbled in Sophie's chest. She snaked a hand to Carla's and gripped it tight.

"I'm proud of you, Sophie, for how hard you've worked to help provide for Mom. And I know you're in a state of transition right now, but honey, just go with it. Okay? Things might just work out." Carla held up a finger to indicate a moment, stood, and grabbed something off the counter. She sat again, handing a slip of paper to Sophie. She read it, and then read it again, a hand over her mouth to stifle a laugh-sob that worked its way up. It was an advertisement from a dance academy in Missoula, looking for two full-time instructors. "The woman who owns it works at Roger's firm. I may have told her about you." Carla shot Sophie a look, with a self-satisfied smile.

Sophie was speechless. Nothing would have come out right at that point. With a wink, Carla grabbed another wine bottle from the counter and shoved it at Sophie.

"So, carnival cowboy…"

Sophie wiped at her eyes and set the wine bottle between her thighs. "Yeah, he...we, it's over. Nothing to talk about there." Right? Because talking about Tucker wasn't going to take back what he'd said yesterday, or the rock in her gut, or the way she loved him so completely despite it all.

"I'm assuming you're having sex with him?"

"Incredible sex," Sophie uttered, then snorted a laugh as she took a sip. TMI. Carla shook her head.

"If you were to take the *incredible* sex away, would you still want him?"

Sophie didn't even have to think about the answer to that. She'd take Tucker anyway she could have him. His laugh, his crooked smirk. The irritating toothpick. How he made her laugh and the way he held her hand and protected her from man-eating squirrels. She'd take it all.

"God, yes."

"Then I'd say that's as close to love as you can get." Carla nodded to prove her point and Sophie drained her wine glass. They sat in silence again, eyeballing the amazing amount of dust bunnies under the refrigerator. "Before we start destroying my beautiful kitchen, I need to tell you." Carla popped the top on the second wine bottle. "The convalescent center received a generous donation. Sophie, Mom's entire medical bill was paid."

• • •

Tucker walked into the training arena to find Jim Gilfoyle holding a set of blueprints and staring at the ceiling. He turned as Tucker's boots crunched over the sand floor and grinned like he'd been expecting him.

"Tucker, what do you think about the peak on these prints compared to the way this building is done?" Jim let one side of the prints fall as he pointed to the skylights. Tucker had come in to look for a pair of nippers he'd set down earlier, not to discuss construction plans. He was so tore up inside and pissed off at himself that nothing seemed right. The world was off its fucking center.

"Don't matter much." He kept on walking.

"Tucker," Jim's voice was light, but firm. "How long have we known each other?" Tucker stopped but didn't look back and he didn't answer. The sound of rustling paper told him Jim was rolling the prints. He set his shoulders. There wasn't a single ounce in his body that wanted to have a conversation with Jim Gilfoyle right now. He loved Jim, more than he'd loved his own father, likely, but for some reason, being next to him at the moment was rubbing him wrong. Really wrong.

"You were three when I invested my first million here. Do you know why I did that?"

Tucker turned. "No."

"Because I loved your mother. And I loved you, and your brothers. Cooper made a few bad decisions on the best place to put Paint River's budding money. He damn near lost the ranch, so I stepped in."

Tucker kept his voice neutral. "How noble of you." Being as ass to Jim was about as low as he could get, but hell, he was already crawling on his belly, so what the hell.

Jim sighed and stepped closer. "Paint River is in a good place now, Tucker. It can be whatever you want it to be." Jim touched his shoulder. Tucker's muscles flinched at the contact, but he stopped himself before flinging Jim off. "Tuck, I just want to take care of your mother."

Tucker twisted away. He took several paces to create some distance. Take care of Maeve? He'd been doing that for so long, Tucker couldn't fathom not being the one she leaned on. He was good at holding her up—at holding them all up. When Levi secretly confessed he was leaving for the Marines because he hated ranching, Tucker kept his brother's secret and helped him go through with his decision. When his little niece Birdie cried, Tucker was there to make it better. He was always there. Watching. Protecting. Supporting.

And they'd moved on to find love and, in a way, start over. He should be doing that, but instead, he'd driven Sophie away because he didn't know how to keep her. He didn't know how to not be angry inside, or feel like he was doing well enough. He didn't know how to support her through the ups and downs; watch her cry, make it better. Tucker glanced at the ceiling with the urge to scream, "Thanks for being a role model, Dad," but of course, he didn't.

Jim continued gently, "I'm going to marry your mother and I was hoping for your blessing."

Tucker spotted the nippers, picked them up, and palmed them. He bounced their weight in his hand. "You have my blessing. But I want to know one thing." He wanted to throw the nippers as hard and fast as he could and absorb the sound as they impacted against the wall because that's about how his soul felt right now. Slammed, shattered.

Jim's face was a little pale—gray, maybe—when he looked into his eyes. "Why'd you wait so long?"

The older man spread his hands wide. "What do you mean?"

Wasn't it pretty obvious?

"I needed you. We all needed you...do you know what a difference it would have made to have you in our lives instead of that piece of shit," his voice trailed off, his entire body shaking. The ground was calling to him, begging the sudden weakness in his legs to just bring him down. "I'd have been a better man with you in his place." Jim's face went another shade paler, and Tucker felt immediate regret. It was true, he'd thought about it all the time when he was younger, having Jim as a father. Still, that boyhood wish had no business coming out the mouth of a man.

"Tucker, I couldn't be more proud of the man you are than if I had been your father. I loved you all—I still do, but it wasn't my place to step in. I respected your mother's marriage, and we never walked over the vows she'd made. I was there for you the best I could be then and I'm here for you now, Tuck."

Tucker looked away. Sophie was out of reach now, or should be, after what he'd said to her. It was for the best, no matter how his soul raged that he was wrong.

"Yeah, well, it's too late."

Jim stood there for several moments before giving a resigned nod and walking away. Tucker waited until Jim exited the arena before letting out the burn of pent up breath. He should be happy for his mother—glad that she found happiness with a man who radiated his love for her. It didn't matter how many times he stabbed at the truth to make it bleed and go away. He was jealous of the love everyone else seemed to have but him.

. . .

Sophie nodded a greeting to Jim Gilfoyle as she walked into the stable and he walked out. The smell of hay was sweet and mixed with the headier aroma of horses and leather, creating a fragrance Sophie would be able to taste on her tongue and relive in her mind at will once she left here. There was a lot about Paint River she was going to miss; the most potent aspect of the ranch being somewhere within the stable walls.

She'd steeled herself for coming face-to-face with Tucker after he'd shot her down. Her pride wouldn't let her get away with not having this conversation with him. Despite the resolve she told herself that she had, Sophie was a ball of nerves. She walked the length of the aisle, taking her time to peek in the occupied stalls. Tucker's horse was second from the last on the left and, despite having fresh hay, he was alone inside. She peeked in at Pana in the last stall. He dozed with his head in the corner, his ears flicking when she clicked her tongue at him. The connecting door to the arena bounced open as Tucker stormed through it. His eyes were fixed ahead, shadowed by the scowl on his brow. He didn't even notice her by Pana's stall as he walked past with huge, purposeful strides.

A flicker of anxiety jetted inside her, but she pushed it aside. "Tucker?"

His head snapped to the right as he faltered a little and swiveled to look back at her. There was no welcome in his face; there was no readable expression at all. Suddenly, the pie in her hands felt incredibly heavy and incredibly silly.

"Is this a bad time?"

His jaw jerked. "Yep." The distance in his eyes was a blatant warning to stay out of his zone, and as much as she wanted to listen, Sophie wanted to breech it more. When he tipped his head up and looked down his nose at her, he was formidable, and she ached to see it. Sophie looked down to get away from the intensity of his face.

He started walking away. "Follow me."

He stormed into the office, holding the door for her before shutting it hard. Tucker whipped off his hat, one hand raking through his hair while the other popped the buttons on his shirt. Sophie remained quiet as he stripped off his shirt and threw it down on top of the hat. He pulled the neck of his T-shirt and rotated his shoulders as if everything was suddenly too small.

"What do you need?" He didn't look at her. Instead, Tucker opened the office window to let the slight breeze in, then turned the pole fan on and pointed it at the desk. After a second, he adjusted it again. Then he stared at it with hands on his hips and a steely set to his shoulders.

Sophie set the pie on the desk. "It was you...wasn't it?"

He didn't look at her. "What was me?"

"You...you're my mother's benefactor."

Tucker turned, hands still on his hips. He looked into space like he was lost. "Okay."

"Okay?" She touched her fingers to the edge of the desk. A mere three feet separated them, but it felt like the entire Northern Hemisphere lay in divide. "That's an odd choice of response. Anyway, I came to say thank you. You have no idea what this means—"

Tucker flicked a hand at her. "Don't, Sophie." He leaned forward as if bracing for a physical blow. Without his hat and gloves, stripped down to his jeans and T-shirt, he looked raw and slightly vulnerable. His tone was anything but.

Sophie shuddered. Her throat burned, but she forced words out. "I'll find a way to repay you." She crossed her arms tight over her chest and took a small step back. The door handle pressed into her butt, making her jerk.

Tucker scoffed. He pinched his nose with his thumb and middle finger. "That's a nice thought, Sophie, really, but don't worry about it. Seriously, I would never expect it for one thing, but do you really think you could ever pay that back? Let's be realistic."

Her mouth dropped, anxiety inside blossoming into a rolling boil of anger. "You son of a bitch!" she sputtered. "What is wrong with you?"

He shook his head to dissuade her, or to warn her, she wasn't sure. Didn't care. The hurt inside was too big. No matter how many times his mind told him to stop this, a bigger part of him said he needed to keep driving her away. Self-preservation. It kicked in strong because if he let his guard down for one second, he'd wrap her in his arms and beg for forgiveness. Truthfully, he was so damn scared of what he'd see in her eyes, so he pushed this distance between them.

"We donate to charity all the time. This was no different. You don't pay back charity."

"My mother is not a charity case!" Now she just wanted to kill him, grab the trophies off the bookshelf behind the desk and pommel him.

Tucker's face was pained, like he was trying to hold back the devil himself. "You're right, she's not." He spread his arms wide, lips tight. "But come on, Sophie. All those hours at the bar for what? Was it really going to get you anywhere?" He spun on one heel to look out the window. Sophie's eyelids fluttered. Her chest ached like he'd punched her and rammed a fistful of hay down her throat. Before she could speak, before she could process or think, Tucker spun back. His left hand came down in a fist on the desk, jerking her senses out of stupor.

"Tucker," his name was a breathy accusation, the strongest she could manage. She reached a hand on the desk to steady herself. Her fingers hit the edge of the pie plate, flipping it over the side and onto the floor. It made a loud echo on the cement as peaches splattered Tucker's leg. She looked down at the mess, chest heaving as a numb kind of panic slowly pumped its way over her nerves. An inner voice welled inside, demanding to have its say, but she couldn't produce the words. Sophie grappled behind her for the door handle, managed to crack the door just enough that she could back out of it. Eyes on the peaches, she slipped out, flicking her gaze to meet his cold eyes for just a second before she shut the door.

• • •

Tucker wouldn't give in to the urge to sit, or worse, collapse. Hitting the wall until his knuckles split seemed like a good idea—he could already feel the crack of skin, and burn of bone against solid wood—but he wouldn't give in to that either. He forced himself to stand completely still and watch Sophie's expression as she backed out of the door. The shock, the hurt, no, the *agony*, on her face was his doing and he'd take the repercussions face-on. It was never his intention to paint that raw emotion on her face, but he'd done it anyway. Another fail.

Cool wetness seeped through the denim just below his knee where peach juice bled through. Chest heaving, Tucker looked down at the mess: a fancy, enamel, cream-colored pie plate with red rim, an embroidered flour sack towel, and a mash of orange goo and crust lay at the tips of his boots. She'd made him a goddamn peach fucking pie. And he'd implied she was a charity case, had made her feel like nothing.

Knees aching, lungs heaving, Tucker let air in and out through his nose, and tried to force all the emotions away. In his mind, a big black cloud appeared over his head. Let it rain down on him and pour Sophie's memory over him until he drowned in her. With each drop, he'd be baptized in the reality of what a piece of shit he really was.

Absently, he slid the pie tin over with the tip of a boot and shook peaches from his pants leg. Turning, he slowly buckled his chaps back on and slid into his hat and gloves. His cell rang from its place in his back pocket, but he ignored it as he paused to stare at nothing in particular. It was the opportunity he needed to shove thoughts of Jim and his mother and Sophie to the back of his brain and get his head back into work.

His cell rang again as he stepped out of the office. Tucker growled. Half the time there was no reception and now, when he least wanted to talk to anyone, it rang non-stop. Tucker stomped down to Pana's stall, his lips set in a determined line. Nothing would feel better than having a go-around with a twelve-hundred-pound mass of angry muscle. Pana's ass was to the door. The horse turned his neck lazily to look when Tucker reached through the bars and slapped him on the butt. Jesus, even Pana seemed depressed. Tucker glared at the horse. Hell, maybe he'd broken Pana, too.

"Tucker!"

He turned as Jaxon ran down the aisle, waving his arms. He made it about halfway when he hunched over panting. "Jesus, answer...your damn...phone!"

Every hair on the back of Tucker's neck went electric. "What's wrong?"

Jax stood and waved Tucker down the aisle. "Jim. It's Jim. He's not breathing!"

Chapter Twenty

He'd thought the pain he felt over hurting Sophie was excruciating, but Tucker was in no way prepared for the onslaught of gut-wrenching emotion he experienced when he saw Jim Gilfoyle lying in the grass. Maeve knelt by Jim's head, talking to him in broken, tear-filled words.

Sophie was on her knees next to Jim, the first-aid kit from the bunk house at her side, her arms straight with elbows locked and hands fisted together. Jim's shirt was bunched up around his throat as Sophie pressed the heel of her clasped hands down on his chest. She counted to herself each time she used her own body weight to compress his chest, up and down, and up and down. Tucker heard her soft voice, and the refractory sound of muscle, tendon, and bone trying to resist the pressure.

Several people were gathered around, but Tucker could only see Sophie and Maeve. There was a piece of plastic in Jim's mouth, a medical device of some kind, his skin milky pale in contrast to his usual sun-loving tan. Tucker stopped near Sophie's leg, too scared to get any closer. Maeve looked up at him and the mask on her face let lose. Tucker hurried to her as she stood and grabbed his shirt. She buried her face in his chest, her tears soaking the fabric in a flood. He closed his eyes against the whimpered sounds of her pain. "Ma."

"Thirty-two years, Tucker." She heaved a huge breath. "I waited thirty-two years and now I'm going to lose him!" His chest was so constricted, he couldn't breathe, couldn't think. Tucker's gaze latched onto Sophie as she alternated between chest compressions and breathing into Jim's mouth through the plastic tube. Strain etched the lines of her face, but she looked determined and unsure, and Tucker realized she was doing everything she could to save Jim's life.

"Jaxon," Sophie called out. He hurried to her. "Can you drive out to the field there with your flashers on?" She stopped compressions, slid her hand along Jim's neck. Sweat rolled off her forehead, her arms shaking. "The helicopter will be here in about six...holy shit, I have a pulse."

Maeve's head snapped up. "What?"

Sophie looked down, eyes closed with her fingers pressed against Jim's neck. After a second, she nodded with a relieved smile. "Yeah." She dug around in the kit and grabbed a stethoscope. After *shhing* everyone, she listened to Jim's chest. Tucker could see a soft rise and fall of Jim's chest, but it seemed too slow to be doing any good. Maeve slid to Jim's side and took his face in her hands, talking to him softly. Tucker put a hand on her shoulder. His gaze slid to Sophie several times, but she never met his eyes, never even looked his way.

When she resumed compressing Jim's chest, Maeve got frantic again.

"You said he had a pulse!"

Sophie nodded, focused again on what she was doing. "Not enough. I have to keep...helping him...until the bird gets here. Keep...talking to him."

Maeve's gray hair bobbed as she spoke to Jim, her shoulders hunched in defeat. She'd cried when Cooper died, but not like this. Tucker tilted his head a little with the realization. Her grief then had been quiet and internal. Most of her tears had been shed in private, he supposed, since she'd cried very little in front of him. This sorrow was the grief of a woman losing a lover and a best friend. This grief was consuming her and squeezing out the part of her soul that had no desire to live without it's other half. In his thirty-one years, Tucker couldn't recall a single incident in which Maeve had lost her composure the way she was losing it now. Her only reason for existing at this moment was to comfort Jim back into life or into death, whichever way nature took things. It was a pure, unadulterated love and Tucker hoped the devil would drag him straight to hell before letting Maeve lose that now.

The helicopter came, followed by a flurry of activity. The flight medics conversed with Sophie while they put Jim on a white board and hooked him up to equipment. There were needles and tubes and little vials of medicine, and then the medic patted Sophie on the back and shook her hand, and they were gone. Sophie stood behind the house, watching the helicopter leave, her arms crossed tight. When Maeve rushed her and wrapped her arms around Sophie's head and clung to her, Sophie clung right back. Tucker looked away as the two women he cared about the most cried together.

He waited in silence until Maeve came over and took his hand.

"I'll drive you, Ma. Missoula General?"

She nodded with a wan smile. "He had a good pulse and was breathing on his own by the time they left." She looked up with hopeful eyes. "Thanks to Sophie."

• • •

Jim had a balloon inserted in an artery and a stent placed to keep blood flowing, and after four hours of surgery and a million moments of sadness and worry, Maeve smiled again. As much as Tucker ached, he knew he'd never had a choice whether to let his mother go into Jim's arms or not. She was simply, quietly, waiting for his blessing, but she'd move on no matter if he gave it or not. And now his bitter words had thrown Jim into this hospital bed.

Stepping into Jim's dimly lit room, surrounded by the sounds of medical equipment, Tucker found Maeve sitting in a chair next to the bed. He recalled how Birdie had been kicked by Pana bar Noir a year before, and fought for her life in a room like this one—how he'd had to hold Cole down to keep him from destroying the place from grief. But Maeve sat with her usual quiet strength, and Tucker was amazed at how differently they all handled grief and stress. He usually just walked away, but not now. He couldn't leave her. Swallowing hard, Tucker walked up behind Maeve and put his hands on her shoulders. He kissed the top of her head as her hands came up to slide over his.

"Ma, this is my fault…"

"Don't even think that, Tucker," Maeve whispered softly. Tucker dropped to a crouch beside Maeve's chair. She read his thoughts so well. "There's nothing to apologize for."

"There is." He squeezed his eyes shut. "Jim…came to see me earlier. Asked for my blessing and…I wasn't nice about it." He glanced at Jim's still form on the bed. Hooked up to monitors and wires and tubes, he looked like someone else— anyone but the sturdy, vital man Jim had always been. "If I hadn't gotten him angry, this wouldn't have…"

Maeve shook her head and pressed a hand to Tucker's cheek. "Sweetheart, no, no. This isn't your fault. This isn't anyone's fault. Jim's been getting tests for the past couple weeks because he's been so tired. A blood clot blocked an artery—this would have happened no matter what."

"He's a good man." Tucker glanced at the floor. "He's always been a good man, and if he's what you want, I'll give you my blessing for all it's worth. I just want you to have what you need." Maeve's tears fell with a slow slide over her cheeks.

"What do *you* need, Tuck?" She squeezed his shoulder like she could erase the knots of all his pain from over the years. Her fingers moved in a familiar dig and release into the muscle, the way she'd done since he was a kid to try and help him relax. It was soothing now just as it had been then.

"I need you to be happy. I need Jim to get better. I *need* Paint River." He met Maeve's gaze and the distraught gleam in her eyes cut him deep.

"You're forgetting something."

"No," Tucker said. "I'm not." He rose and hugged Maeve around the neck. She looped her arms over his and clung to him, her chest shuddering with tear-filled breaths. Paint River would always need him, and as far as Tucker was concerned, he could never set foot off the property again and be perfectly happy. That's all he *wanted*.

Tucker pulled away and handed Maeve a tissue from a box on the rolling table next to him. He stood. "I'll wait in the family room until you're ready to go."

"No, no. I'm staying the night. The nurse said that it's fine."

"Then I'll stay with you a while." Tucker passed the time between pacing the family room, getting numerous cups of coffee, and standing in the hallway watching medical staff walk back and forth. The cardiologist came, reassured them that Jim was doing as well as could be expected, and would likely wake up any time. Tucker was just walking out of Jim's room when Jaxon met him in the hall. Hat in his hand, his friend waved a little sheepishly.

"How's he doing?"

Tucker slapped Jaxon on the shoulder. "Holding his own." Jaxon nodded with a pleased smile, but his shoulders were slumped and stiff.

"You want to tell me what's up?" A little flag of warning waved in front of Tucker's face when Jaxon's lips went tight and pinched.

"I...just brought Sophie to town. Her ma..." Jaxon blinked twice. "Her ma is dying and she was too upset to drive herself in." Tucker's skin screamed like he'd been doused with ice water. His muscles jerked, but he caught himself before he could race down the hall. This didn't concern him. This shouldn't concern him, especially after the way he'd tore her down. He glanced at Maeve. Sophie wouldn't grieve with quiet grace; she'd suffer. All the months she'd spent in constant fear would come to a head. An image of her curled up on the floor flashed through his mind and his neck tensed with excruciating force.

"I can't go."

It was Jaxon's turn to touch Tucker's shoulder. Their eyes met. The profound understanding in Jaxon's eyes wasn't comforting; it just made him doubt himself more.

"Say something!" Tucker barked, pulling away from Jaxon's touch and turning his back. Tucker tapped a knuckle against his lips, waiting for Jax to speak, wasn't surprised when he didn't. "She's not mine to worry about." He paced half the length of the hall, crushed the brim of his hat between fingers that couldn't stop moving. Spinning, nearly crashing into a nurse, Tucker stomped back, grabbed Jaxon's shirt and brought them nose to nose. Jax stood stoic, his eyes soft.

"I can't go!" He stared at Jax long and hard for one heart beat, two, before ripping himself away and running down the hall.

Chapter Twenty-One

Sophie was three pounds, two ounces when she was born. No matter how many times Violet retold Sophie's birth story over the years, one thing never changed: the raw undertone of fear in her eyes when she spoke about how small and frail Sophie had been, how each breath was like the flutter of a butterfly, bringing hope that, despite the odds, her small body would blossom. That fear was never masked by a smile or twinkle in Violet's eye. Every retelling seemed to invoke the same sense of desperate unknowing—wondering if at any moment her fragile baby was going to die.

The sound of Violet's labored breathing was the only noise in the room. And as Sophie clutched the blue seersucker fabric of her mother's nightgown, she was positive the emotion inside her was the same that Violet had experienced then— the urgent, primal need to hang on to the one she loved, to encourage her to fight for life. It was a love passed from Violet's womb to Sophie's soul, and as she felt her mother's breaths rise and fall against her knuckles, Sophie knew that was the greatest gift she ever gave.

The nurse had come in earlier and gave Violet a light sponge bath, wiping away the vestiges of her body's attempt to purge itself as death slowly sank in. She'd been cleaned with fresh soap and powder, but all Sophie could smell was an undertone of Red Door perfume, the scent her mother had put on everyday for as long as Sophie could recall. In the past two hours, Violet's breathing had slowed, her skin chilled like winter's kiss. In the past few minutes, the pound of her jugular had slowed until it was undetectable against the translucent skin of her neck. Sophie gently wiped away residue from her mother's lips, but no matter how many times she wiped, it just kept coming.

It was time. And Sophie was nowhere near ready.

Carla sat beneath the big bay window, her knees drawn to her chest and forehead against them. She hadn't looked up in so long, Sophie thought she'd maybe passed out from stress, but she was too drained to ask or to care. With shaking fingers, Sophie rubbed the back of Violet's hand. The loose skin bunched and slid under the contact, ropey veins rolling out of the way. Sophie felt each knobby finger, each knuckle, each tip of every fingernail. Violet's hands were beautiful, even now. They were giving hands, working hands, loving hands, and she'd miss their touch until her last days.

She studied her mother's face. Those eyes had looked at her with so much love and adoration. They'd been forgiving, no matter what Sophie had done wrong, no matter what horrible thing teenage angst made her say or do. Those lips smiled with more warmth than the sun as Sophie grew and accomplished and succeeded. No matter what was wrong, no matter what was right, Sophie looked to Violet's face for reassurance. Even now, in the last whispers of life, Violet's beautiful face was exactly what she needed.

A soft sound behind her made Sophie turn. She expected the nurse, but Tucker's big body claimed the doorway, hat in his hands, his eyes full of despair. Sophie sobbed and looked away. Anguish and relief were twins inside her. Rubbing her forehead, she managed a breath.

"What are you doing here?"

He took a step, his boot crunching softly on the wooden floor. "Sophie." It was a plea, an offering, a condolence. She couldn't do it, not now. Sophie hung her head in her heads and heaved a breath.

"Please go."

He came forward a little more. "Soph."

"No!" She swiveled in her chair, her voice a desperate hiss. "Please, please go." Violet made a gurgling sound, drawing Sophie back. Violet's lips gasped, her entire chest rising off the mattress and slumping back down. Sophie shook her head.

She knew.

"Carla!" Desperation cut her in half. This couldn't be happening. Not for real. For months, death was a possibility that never came. Today shouldn't be the day.

Sophie grabbed a box of tissue from the stand and threw it at Carla. It hit her in the top of the head. "Please don't make me do this alone." Her sister's head snapped up, eyes huge like she was seeing the room for the first time. Without a word, she scrambled to her feet and raced to the bathroom, slamming the door. *Click*.

Wiping her face with one hand, Sophie stood over her mother. She touched Violet's belly and gave her a little pat. "Mom, please. Not today. Don't do this today." She dropped the rag and put both hands on Violet's chest, gripping and smoothing the nightgown.

"Tomorrow, all right? Not today. We'll do this tomorrow. Stay with me one more day. Please, Mom...please." Sophie sunk to the mattress, her forehead leaning on Violet's chest. Rise and fall. The smell of phantom perfume and soap permeating the air as the rise and fall shuddered. Then stopped.

"I can't...I can't..." Sophie choked, her knees wobbling to hold her in place against the bed. She shook Violet's chest, suddenly more alone than she'd ever felt in her life. Huge tears punched her eyes, clogging her nose and throat and suffocating her in salty grief. "Mom..."

Alone.

"Tucker!" His name squeaked from her lips, the sound of it forcing out the longing she'd been holding inside. He'd already left, was probably long gone. Sophie lost her legs, slid to the floor to the sound of racing boots. And then he was there, his strong arms bringing her up against his chest as she clung to him. And cried.

• • •

Sophie leaned over and touched Violet's cheek with a lingering kiss, and Tucker knew he'd never be the same. In the hours that passed, he'd convinced Carla to come out of the bathroom, helped Sophie fill out some paperwork, called Carla's husband to come get her, and held Sophie's hand while she and Carla said a final good-bye.

They hadn't spoken much and that was all right. There weren't any words that would be good enough. Silence was like a salve, or so he hoped, as Sophie lost a couple battles with tears, composed herself, and sunk into the same cycle again. She'd collapsed with her head on his lap as he drove them to Paint River. Tucker slid his fingers through her hair, hoping it comforted her a little, and by the soft, steady sound of her breathing, thought it probably had.

Emotions were fickle and they'd ganged up on him like a twin tornado. He didn't know how to respond to the depths of grief the women in his life had gone through today. That they seemed to welcome his presence made him feel like he'd done something to help, and in that, Tucker allowed himself some give. But for the bitter words he'd said to Sophie, he gave himself hell. Looking down at her still form, Tucker wanted to apologize, to ask for her forgiveness. When the time felt right, he would, if he could think of the right words to say.

Tucker parked in front of the ranch house. He sat and stared out the windshield for long moments, running his hands through Sophie's hair. She was sound asleep and, though he hated to wake her, Tucker roused her with a gentle shake. Sophie sat up with a blank stare and rubbed her face. And burst into quiet sobs. Tucker went to the passenger door and gently pulled her out, cradling her in his arms as he walked up the porch steps and into the empty house.

Her arms embraced his neck as he bypassed the couch, and took her to his room. He clicked on the bedside lamp and lay Sophie on the neatly made bed. He went to the attached bathroom and grabbed a tissue. Sophie was curled up on her side when he hurried back. Her soft sobs tugged at his heart and chipped away at his strength.

Kicking off his boots, Tucker lay down facing her, smoothed hair away from her face and dabbed tears away from her cheeks. Her small hands gripped his shirt as she pulled herself closer until Tucker had her completely wrapped up in his arms. His cheek to the top of her head, her leg thrown over his thigh, his hand making small circles on her back. The weight of her body next to his on the mattress was a delicious sensation.

Night deepened the room, lulling Tucker into a half sleep. Soft pressure against his chest roused him a little, warmth sliding along his chest sending warm flutters over his skin. The sensation poured over his abdomen and along his ribs, tracing along his pecs and over his collarbone. Pleasure eased him awake. His eyes fluttered open to see Sophie staring at him in the soft glow of lamplight.

Tucker sucked in a long breath as Sophie's hands pushed up under his shirt and cupped the column of his throat. He leaned up on his elbows, reached across his body and pulled the shirt over his head. Sophie mumbled something as her cheek slid onto his chest. Her right hand trailed lazily over his flesh, stopping to trace each contour, each dip and line of muscle. It might have been minutes or hours, he didn't know, didn't care as he surrendered to the simple pleasure of her touch. He was completely, undeniably in love with her. No denying it, no sense in trying.

Her lips pressed against his ribs as she murmured, "So much more than I imagined."

Tucker grabbed her hand in his, brought her knuckles to his lips as their eyes met. He couldn't disassemble the sadness from the longing in her eyes. When she moved over him and pressed her lips to his neck, he hoped that this is what forgiveness felt like. Sophie straddled him, placing his face between her warm hands.

Tucker grabbed her elbows. "Sophie…"

She pressed a finger to his lips, pleading with her eyes. No talking. Just take it all away. He relaxed and sank into the pillow. Her mouth followed him down, kissing and nipping at his jaw, his neck, over his collarbone. Tucker shivered, gripping her hips with a groan. His body melted under the ministrations of her mouth and her hands.

He willed his body to stay still and relaxed while Sophie traced and kissed every inch of his chest. She massaged his biceps and ran her palms down the length of his forearms before curving in to the waist of his jeans. All the best whiskey in Paint River's basement couldn't produce a drunk like this. The button popped on his jeans, the zipper released and Sophie's warm hands slipped inside. Tucker's head lolled back against the pillow. When her fingernails dragged over his groin, he lay back with a groan and pulled her up against the length of his body. Their mouths met softly and tension melted from Sophie's muscles. She swayed into him, stroking his neck and shoulders with slow hands.

There was a line about to be crossed. He could feel it, but he didn't know what it was. Even in her grief, she needed him and he wasn't going to deny her. He may never be anything more for Sophie than a distraction, but for right now, it would be enough. And when he set foot over that line and the truth became crystal clear, he'd take the consequences. Whatever they may be.

Love ran deep, even if it meant an imperfect ending.

In an instant, their clothes lay in a mess at the end of the bed. Never taking his eyes from her face, Tucker smoothed his hands over her body, memorizing the feel of her supple curves. He kissed every inch he could reach, pounding the taste of her into his mind and locking it away while he willed her scent to become a permanent perfume.

Sophie straddled him and bent her lips to his skin. Having her like this, her hands and lips and soul on him, could happen every day and never be enough. She bit his neck with tender nips while she lowered herself over him, taking his cock in one steady slide inside her body. Every movement was unhurried and savored, giving them time to commit these moments to memory and lock them away. The room began to swirl as Tucker stroked Sophie in the way he knew made her unravel. Her soft moans turned into a ragged announcement of flight, and she carried him away with her. Tucker released in an ecstatic burst at the same time her inner muscles clamped hard and she cried his name.

He could barely breathe, thought he might be suffocating from the force of his own feelings. Sophie collapsed against him, her breath on his neck. Entwined, captured, they held each other as Tucker accepted he would never fully recover. Her breathing steadied and slowed. His heart didn't stop racing. She breathed a sleepy moan.

Trailing a finger over her spine, Tucker pressed his lips to her cheek. "You have me, Fifi. You'll always have me." He succumbed to the lull of exhaustion to the sound of four words against his skin.

"I love you, Tucker."

When he woke in the morning, Sophie had left and her cabin was cleaned out.

Gone.

Chapter Twenty-Two

Sophie put a hand to her stomach and took a long drink of cold water. The bar was packed and she was nowhere near ready to be in the middle of it. Hiding behind the bar for a few minutes gave her some reprieve, but knowing she had to go back out into the herd made her heart race. The internal pilot light that kept her fire going was long cold. No matter how many times her ass got grabbed or patrons tried to raze and jibe her, Sophie didn't have it in her to play back. Everyone got a basic smile, a polite hello, and that was all she could muster.

Her time at the Tap was winding down. She'd accepted a job at the dance academy in Missoula just the day before. Figured it was time to test the waters and see if she could make a go of things here. The plan was a good one and she was satisfied with it…somewhere, beneath the grief. Fred ran a hand over her back in a friendly tickle. "How you doing, kid?" The piercing in his tongue caught and threw the light.

"Fine." She wasn't one to usually understate how she was feeling, but a firm sense of denial was the only thing keeping her sane at the moment. Her mother's ashes sat in an urn above Carla's fireplace, and though they'd been together nearly every day since Violet's death, they hadn't really spoken. There'd been no funeral, no wake. That was what Violet wanted, which left Sophie and her sister to lean on each other. She knew each of them had to deal with the loss of their mother in their own way.

Almost two weeks had passed since her last night with Tucker, but she still felt him under her hands each night when she slipped under the covers. Despite the intimacy he'd shared by letting her touch him, the hurt and reality of his harsh words stayed with her. She loved him, yes, but how was she supposed to navigate the waters with so much uncertainty in her heart? Maybe he loved her; maybe he never really had. She'd been too broken and too numb to stay and find out the morning after Violet died.

Sophie lifted the bar gate as the band tuned up. The band had two female dancers as part of their show, both in tops shorter than the one Sophie wore, with shorts that were little more a denim thong. Every man in the bar was wedged in front of the stage. Just as the lights fell, Sophie heard her name. She looked up into brilliant turquoise eyes. Momentarily stunned by their beauty, she quickly realized the rest of the man was just as gorgeous. Tall, broad physique. Hard, square jaw and chin, straight nose with a blunt tip, slightly downturned eyes. An upper lip that jutted up a little. A flush crept over her at the same time a smack of familiarity hit her.

"Sophie Miller?" The man extended a hand. She didn't take it.

"Yes?"

He looked extremely pleased with himself. "Cole Haywood. Nice to meet you." Sophie leaned back so far on her heels she almost tipped over. She grabbed a chair to steady herself. Tucker's brother. He hitched a crooked smile that mirrored Tucker's and a well of fresh grief bubbled inside her.

"I had to come meet the woman who *finally* broke my brother." He looked like this was the best possible thing that could ever come out of his mouth. Sophie wanted to sit down.

"Br-broke?"

Cole swiped a hand in the air. "Yeah. It's amazing. For the first time, my smart-ass, cocky, talks-back, self-centered son-of–a-bitch brother has nothing to say. *Nothing*. He's quiet and moping and hides out in the woodshop most of the day." Cole gave a satisfied nod." I'd say he's a broken man. And it's a beautiful thing."

Sophie gaped at the lighthearted way he uttered the words. "He's not broken," she said.

Cole lightly touched her arm and leaned in close to her ear. "He misses you. Talk to him. Please?" His face was serious when he pulled back and Sophie saw the worry there. Cole Haywood had a commanding presence and didn't seem the type to go scurrying around trying to fix his brother's messes. For him to be here meant something.

She spread her hands wide with a ragged sigh. "I have nothing to offer him."

Deep understanding darkened those amazing turquoise eyes. Cole's lips turned down in sympathy. "You do or he wouldn't be this damn quiet. And as much as I love not having Tucker arguing with me constantly, I miss my brother. If you don't want him, give him a proper good-bye. If you do, give him a proper hello." Cole smiled warmly as he waited for her response. Sophie could tell he was a man used to being answered, but she could only manage a short nod of understanding.

"If you have time, you might want to stop by the old bridge early tomorrow morning."

The bridge, where she'd first began the free fall into

Tucker. Tears flashed her eyes. She shrugged bonelessly. "I can't."

Cole stared at her a moment. "Well then, that's a damn shame." And he was gone.

• • •

Since Violet's death, Sophie had experienced a slow, almost methodical release of tension that left her almost euphoric with a new weightlessness. Each day, a new muscle group seemed to loosen, a different area of her body would relax, and her mind lightened a little more. She imagined it was because Violet had taken all her pain with her, a mother's final act of love.

She approached the covered bridge as the sun made a full ascent over the trees. Cole Haywood had said to come early, but she'd been unclear what early meant exactly. And with no intentions of actually coming anyway, she hadn't bothered to ask. But here she was and she'd never expected to see the hand-carved sign hanging above the entrance.

JULY PASS

Heart pounding, Sophie approached and stood just inside the mouth of the bridge. The water beneath was higher, thanks to the recent rain, and trickled over the stones and rocks with calming melody. A beam of sunlight caught her attention where it shone like a spotlight on the floor. Sophie squinted against what she thought she saw, and stepped inside a little farther just to be sure.

The floorboard on the threshold had writing on it. *Carnivals are awesome.* Looking down the length of the bridge, Sophie saw that every other floorboard had been replaced to create a pattern of old, dark wood and new, pine-colored planks. All of the new planks contained writing.

She hurried inside, reading them as she walked. *Squirrels*

are the devil. She caused fireworks in my heart. I love her. Tears hit her eyes, blurring the word *love* and making it hard to continue. She kept walking: *Horses are not evil. Mmmm, peach pie. A beautiful angel got her wings. ~Fly away, Violet~*

Sobbing, Sophie crouched and ran her fingers over the writing. He'd created a timeline of her stay at Paint River. He'd stolen July, stuffed it inside the Montana time machine and made it stand still. For a man who'd sworn he couldn't feel anything for her, he'd taken hours to create this treasure. For her.

"Fifi?" Tucker stood at the opposite end of the bridge, hat in his hands, a huge golden horse behind him.

"You lied." Sophie crossed her arms and tossed back her hair. It was a show of bravado to cover how hard she was trying not to hope. "You said you didn't feel anything for me. But this…" She lost her words. Tucker twirled the hat in his hands before taking a few, short, halting steps inside the bridge in her direction.

"I didn't know how to be that man." His voice carried just above the rush of the water below. "I still don't…but I want to try. God, Sophie, I want to try."

Her soul lurched as she leaned forward on her knees. Tucker crossed the distance in a rush and lowered to his knees before her. His thumbs swept at her tears and with each one he carried away, her hope grew.

"Tell me how to apologize so it'll matter, Sophie. Tell me how to make it better and I will." She gripped his wrists, trying to get herself under control.

"You…you stole July." Sophie tipped forward until her forehead rest against his chest.

"I didn't want to let you go," he whispered against her hair. "I love you." He hugged her tighter. "You make me better, Sophie. You make all the things I thought I couldn't have, possible. God, I'm going to screw up, but I promise I'll be that man—the one with a kid under each arm and one stuck to each leg who shows them what it means to be loved. And you...you'll never doubt it. Not for a single second."

Sophie pulled back, tried to look at him, but only burst into tears again. Gently, Tucker helped her to her feet. "Please, Fifi, whatever you're looking for...whatever you need to make your life full again, we'll find it. Together." Sophie threw herself into his arms and held on tight. She'd come to Montana struggling under the weight of life, but that weight had started to fall off a chunk at a time, leaving her finally free. Free to start creating that new way, with the man she loved by her side.

"I love you, too," she whispered. He stroked her hair and pressed her tighter against him. Sophie relished his strength and how his embrace seemed created just for her. Tucker kissed her forehead and pulled back, a wicked gleam in his eye.

"So, does this mean I finally have the right to tell you that you're no longer allowed to work at the Tit?"

She laughed. "Oh my god, Tucker."

"Seriously, I'm burning that shirt..."

Sophie whipped his hat off his head, threaded her fingers through his hair and pulled him in. "Just shut up and kiss me."

Acknowledgments

Fans and readers: Thank you so much for the love and support that you've shown for the Paint River Ranch series. Your emails, sweet notes, incredible reviews and overall love really feed my writer's soul and I cherish each and every one of you!

The Paint River Ranch series wouldn't be the same without the guidance, encouragement and general shenanigans provided by my totally kick-butt critique partners who worked on this story with me. Thank you, Tamara, Tristina, Amber and Heather, Melissa K. and Kayti for loving the Haywood boys as much as I do and for helping me stay true to Tucker's heart. As always, to the WrAHM group—you keep me going, always. Thank you for hours of encouragement, pictures of hot cowboys and the absolute sisterhood you provide.

To Cari Quinn and Taryn Elliot and all the Word Wenches Reader Group, I hope you all know how awesome you are. Thank you for letting me share, and for being friends and fans!

A huge hug and kiss for my husband and children for

giving me the time and understanding it takes to be the family of an author. I hope you truly know that you guys will always come first! Thank you to my agent, and the talented Entangled editors and team that have given me the platform to bring Paint River Ranch to life.

About the Author

Elizabeth Otto grew up in a Wisconsin town the size of a postage stamp, where riding your horse to the grocery store, and skinny dipping after school were perfectly acceptable. No surprise that she writes about small communities and country boys. She's the author of paranormal, and hot, emotional, contemporary romance, and has no guilt over frequently making her readers cry. When not writing, she works full-time as an Emergency Medical Technician for a rural ambulance service. Elizabeth lives with her very own country boy and their three children in, shockingly, a small Midwestern town.

Discover more romance from Entangled...

OVER HER WED BODY
a novel by Alexia Adams

Beckett Samuelson can spot a gold digger when he sees one. So when his ailing father announces his engagement to the private nurse he's only known for two months, Beckett has to step in. Before long he realizes he realizes she's the perfect next Mrs. Samuelson. If only he was the intended groom...

HOW NOT TO MESS WITH A MILLIONAIRE
a Mediterranean Millionaires novel by Regina Kyle

Interior decorator Zoe Ryan's life resembles a country song. What's a girl to do? Leave everything behind for a bit...in Italy. When she gets there, she finds a surprise—millionaire restaurateur Dante Sabbatini in the kitchen. In his underwear. Making coffee. It's suddenly not only hot outside... but what is he doing inside, in her temporary kitchen? The very thing, it seems, that she's trying to avoid, and resisting is impossible.

NO PLAYER REQUIRED
a Biggest Little Love Story novel by JoAnn Sky

Billionaire casino magnate Rafael "Rafa" Salord is forced to exchange caviar for cowboy boots when he's sent to "grow up" and run his father's newly acquired casino in the middle of nowhere downtown Reno. When he crosses paths with feisty Destiny Morson, he starts to wonder if that nonsense about love-at-first-sight might actually be true. Maybe it's time to trade in his playboy status and bet on something more.